Dark Chrysalis

Ian D. Hall

Beaten Track
www.beatentrackpublishing.com

Dark Chrysalis

First published 2020 by Beaten Track Publishing
Copyright © 2020 Ian D. Hall

Paperback ISBN: 978 1 78645 425 6

Beaten Track Publishing,
Burscough, Lancashire.
www.beatentrackpublishing.com

For all who stay by your side when others find ways to leave.

Dedicated to Kate Donaldson who held my hand on a
Greyhound bus journey from Cleveland to Pittsburgh.

With ever grateful thanks to Colin Dexter OBE
and friends who urged me onwards.

Contents

Dark
Chrysalis

Chapter One

The Consequences of Nostalgia

The Accused

T HERE IS NOTHING quite like fear to make you feel guilty, and there is nothing that focuses the mind more than the fear of being taken into a small, austere room against your will. You look for comfort, a sense of the everyday to cling to, any reminder of the world outside, a memento, a souvenir your captive may have left out in the open for you to fixate upon, to pick up and stare at whilst the cogs of time play havoc with your nerves, your memory scrambling as you try to motivate your soul to believe that everything will be all right, that there has been a mistake, an error of judgement.

No, there is nothing quite like fear to make you feel guilty.

Put a man in a cell, and in time, you reduce him to a slave, the hope that he will be set free no more than a continuation of punishment, just one more minute, ticking along to an hour, slowly poisoning the mind, corroding the internal reminders of innocence until the realisation hits. You have been guilty all along, perhaps not of the crime of which you have been accused, but of something else, a split second of indiscretion, the currency of a moment in your life that led you to this point, when you either pace up and down in front of the mirror—a partition between you and those acting as your conscience, judge and cynical jury—or you sit it out, eyes closed, mind alert to the sound of the door opening, the hushed breath, the stink of condemnation and conviction entering the room like cheap cologne, hanging in the air, making you gag with concern, all before you even have an opportunity to reason with yourself and remember you have done nothing wrong.

This is a mistake. It surely must be some sort of error, a confusion over names, times and places, a regretful occurrence they will clear up and then I can return to the safety of a cell of my choosing—my office, surrounded by effects, my clock counting out the time until I can leave for the welcoming arms of the next chapter of non-existence and the sanctity of disappointment.

The detective who arrested me at the university looked apologetic, a gentle hand on my shoulder as a younger, brutish, square-jawed and triumphant policeman placed handcuffs on me, tightly gripped, almost cutting off the circulation to my hands. I suspect an element of bondage role-play in the actions of that young policeman; he seemed to let out a groan of satisfaction as he looked me in the eye, submitting me to his will. Or was it that he felt sure I was guilty of the crime, relishing the sense of power and thinking ahead to when his shift finished and he would regale his comrades with how he caught the killer of Samantha Ó Foghladh?

Innocent I may be, but the name I knew, from a long-distant past, the happiest days of my life, to a recent recall of madness when I tried in vain to reach out and find her, sending a letter to the last known address I had and to the local newspaper that covered the area she'd told me she came from. Samantha Ó Foghladh was a woman I had loved since she first smiled at me as I stumbled down the narrow aisle of the Greyhound bus, fleeing the midnight terrors Cleveland had offered this young British lad as he travelled, searching for some secret recipe for the meaning of life.

Samantha Ó Foghladh was a young woman, no older than twenty—part of me suspected she was barely eighteen. The sense of adventure emanated from her as if she bathed in it twice a day. Over the humdrum of others' lack of discourse and embracing of the boredom only a long bus journey can offer, we quickly fell into conversation, one that flowed and took control...*she* took control, laying the groundwork for the man I would become, one who turned his back on the obsolete and saw from her passions that he too could feel something more than antipathy for his fellow man, could share in a dream. It was down to this young woman who had been a dozen places in line before me that my life had changed and was in danger of changing again, twenty-seven years after I first saw her smile.

I realised my eyes had closed. I was concentrating on memories to focus my attention on anything except the starkness of the room in which I was held hostage to nostalgia. Samantha Ó Foghladh had brown hair flecked with blonde that had been dyed in an act of artistic rebellion, small but noticeable, an air of humiliation but self-preservation, denial I had once seen elsewhere in a friend of mine before he disappeared off the grid only to resurface in changing times. Sacrifice and despair haunted the most beautiful smile and determined personality I had ever met.

For a while, for the time it took to travel the darkness between Cleveland and Pittsburgh, I fell hopelessly in love, and it was sealed by a gentle goodbye kiss, a puncture wound that ate at my soul as she boarded another bus to Philadelphia and then on to New York, where she would catch a flight going to Paris to study art by the Seine. Before she left me standing on the dusty sidewalk of Liberty Avenue, I scrawled down an address and placed it somewhere she would eventually see it and think of me. With a wave goodbye from behind the grease-marked window, she slowly rode out of my life; I hoped not forever.

I heard the sound of the door handle turning but kept my eyes closed. Nobody walked in; no smell of accusation sat opposite me. I returned to my thoughts, getting them in order. She asked me of my life, of how I had come so far, far from home, distancing myself from friends, separated by a vast ocean and time. I was shy back then, I still am, sometimes cripplingly so. My former wife complained that I never put myself forward for promotion, always waiting to be asked rather than setting out my goals. It cost me a wife, it cost me job security—saved only the intervention of a friend who put me forward for a position vacated by the death of a senior fellow, one whose name became both famous for his work in the poetic field and infamous for the way his life had been revealed by the local Maltese press to be one of the grotesque masquerading as the highest deception.

Was I as happy on the island as I had been on that bus, surrounded by the unfortunate, the poor, the unsocial, the babes in arms suckling at the rotten fruit of undernourished and unkempt women and the jostling for space between elbows and oversize bags? I am not sure, but I have never met anyone quite like Samantha since.

My time after that encounter was one that bruised along, the life of the nomadic which started by leaving all I knew behind— the quarrels, the floundering recognition of abject direction my life was headed, a couple of weeks spent in the company of good friends in Pittsburgh, a long and blistering hike through Pennsylvania where I met another woman. She became one of the few friends who pushed me as hard as Samantha had, who took me out for dinner in the Dickens Bar and on to New Jersey, where I spent three summer months hanging around Ocean City, getting stoned with the salt of the earth and the indiscreet, the abandoned and the fashionably suited migrant from out of town, the elegant who meandered down from New York looking for expensive memories to share with friends as they returned to the good schools and future university ties, and the down-at-heel, the survivors from Wildwood and the no-hope dreamers of Atlantic City.

I never forgot Samantha, though. Three months of smoking weed and drinking until dawn around hastily constructed bonfires, watching people pair off, break up and start anew, screwing themselves stupid...until death came calling in the summons home. But the responsibility of serious study could not erase the smile of the girl who beckoned me to sit next to her and then filled my mind with hope.

Eventually, I found myself going home, not through some revelation of belonging, of the twang of sorrow for having missed friends and family, but through an arrest. Drunk and stoned, I had waded out into the sea and started throwing things, skimming them against the tide that was threatening to approach, to turn against time. I was told I had howled as the sun dipped away and then, with one last look towards the death of sunset, threw my Walkman into the ocean. I propelled it so far into the damn distance it broke the windscreen of a passing police boat that was patrolling the area. Hardly innocent, I spent the night in jail. Fingerprints taken, I was found to be an illegal alien and deported back to England. No more time, no more excuses, I was guilty of wasting my life and recalled Samantha's words as she confided in me of her purpose, of the journey she was undertaking.

There is movement outside, voices—speaking in Maltese, I guess so as not to give anything away to the suspect. A raised declaration of dissent is expressed, and I figure I don't have much time. Guilty, always guilty of having wasted time.

She was running away, her father was a beast of a man, controlling, fanatical, raging on about how life had screwed him over, that the immigrant was to blame for his faults. Typically mired in steadfast machismo, he was burly, degrading and handy with his fists. She had to get away; she had traded blows too many times, and her sister had offered her a way out, sending money for a plane ticket to Paris and instructions for how to get to New York. A passport gained and a sense of new beginnings ushered into view, she took the chance.

Perhaps this is typical. What teenager doesn't wish to slam the door on their past? What young person filled with resentment and lack of hope doesn't wish to reinvent themselves and find a place where they can make a difference, or at least make peace with their inadequacies and insufficient depth of consumerism?

I had let my mind disappear into the fog of nostalgia, the memory of wanting once more to be held in the gaze of a woman with drive and the will to change her destiny. I had forgotten the reason why I was here: locked in to prevent my mind from escaping, a table and two chairs for company. The ghosts of law and order hover outside the door and on the dark side of the one-way mirror, duplicitous in its attempt to portray that there is more than one soul breathing in the room.

What was this to prove? That I was somehow a living embodiment of Jekyll and Hyde? That inside this shell of a down-beaten man lived the calculating heart of a monster capable of… what? Murder? For that was the sole reason I was here: somehow, Samantha was dead and it was my fault. I hadn't seen her since 1992, not a word from her since that exchange goodbye as the boy racers dragged themselves to immortality along the stretch of road that offered them short life and guest appearances at the morgue as the day turned to forbidding night.

Samantha…who opened my eyes to the wrongs of the world, who gave me a reason to return to my studies and continue in an environment that I felt was killing me and which, in later life, would destroy me. Samantha would have hated to see a once-turned-on mind slowly turning itself off, allowing insecurity to return and slowly but surely descending once more into self-loathing.

Samantha, how can you be dead? I just figured that once you got on that next bus, you had struck up another conversation, found another soul to whom you could give solace and a reason to live. I was fine with that; it never stopped me from believing I might see you again one day, but I was fine…

Who am I kidding? You were the one I needed. That's why I took the plunge and looked for you again—to reach out, even if you were happy. I just needed inspiration to carry on.

The voices are louder now. Time is back on track. Soon, I will be sent home. Soon, memories from my youth spent smoking dope and drinking cheap bourbon and talking animatedly of British rock music and discovering my soul…will be lost. Across the bonfire, I see a face I know, beautiful, haunting, lonely…

and then, like the flames that once burned so brightly, like the tendrils of smoke grasping at the air, it is gone, turned to ash, dreams forgotten in an instant.

I went home. I continued my studies, but because of the pressure on my mind, I required time out before I could strive for a position that would have made Samantha proud of me. The charges against me were applied but never followed through: a friend from the beach persuaded their father to apply a weight of influential opinion ahead of election year. I got lost in a system once; after my studies, I found myself disorientated once more.

How did Samantha die?

They could not, or perhaps would not, answer that. The only conclusion I could discern was that I had sent up some flag by writing to the newspaper. A note of innocent appeal—*I am looking for a friend. She lived in your area and had a sister called Catherine, about eighteen years of age, brown hair with flecks of blonde, I would so like to see her again.* It was either that or the power of the internet. Her name tapped in to no avail, I thought, paying no heed to the colossal amount of data that zipped into view, nothing but internet trash, a seamless trough of possible highlights…too much to cope with.

Had I seen something and dismissed it? Possible. For all my endeavours to be observant, sometimes I skip details that might be important, preferring to fixate on the minute, the moment which grabs my heart. What are they going to tell me when they finally see that I have stopped sweating, that I have cocooned myself against the problem at hand—a coping mechanism taught me whilst I was hidden from public view?

You will be deported, boy. Just be thankful that I am being lenient. Your benefactor has persuaded me that you meant no harm, and while your actions could have caused a potential tragedy, I am led to believe it was down to youthful exuberance. However, son, you are here illegally. You had six months, and you have been here a year. I would hold you until the end of time if it meant I could find out all that you have done since first entering the country. You seem suspicious, boy, you're a troublemaker, boy, you are going to jail one day, boy. The clock is ticking.

I cannot remember all that I did whilst backpacking around America, or why I took off from home. Hell, these days I struggle to remember what I discussed with my students in my office, sometimes covering the same ground, much to the amusement of those who walk through the English Literature classes with me. Somehow, I know that it is important I remember. Any small detail might prove invaluable, might prove I am innocent of the crime…

Of murdering Samantha.

It was then that he walked in. A detective around my age but with sad eyes to match his dishevelled appearance, who had placed a firm but sympathetic hand on my shoulder as I was press-ganged into the service of supposed criminality and blackened name. He introduced himself and spoke to me briefly before calling in another police officer and the state-sponsored lawyer who had been assigned to me. Then he turned on the tape and asked the first of many questions that would leave me reeling.

I counted to ten, then twenty, silently, refusing to speak, unable to believe that I was here, in this small cell, no escape from the nightmare. The other police officer was becoming exasperated with my lack of answers; the lawyer kept silent, making the odd note here and there, scribbling down the inevitable. Only the detective remained calm, as if his sorrow were deeper than mine, his mind in greater turmoil.

It was a further ten minutes before I recognised him and asked him to confirm who he was. "If you tell me, I will tell you all I know," I found myself saying to him, exposing the naked fragility of the conversation at hand.

I was right: he was the detective who was friends with the doctor I had replaced at the university, and he looked tired.

Chapter Two

Same Name, Different Number

The Detective

I FELT LIKE DEATH. Outwardly, I tried to portray the same sense of order I'd once displayed to my fellow officers, the citizens of my country and the visitors who made their way to the island to feel the sunshine on their backs as they lazed away time and found ways to enjoy much-deserved freedom. Inwardly, I saw the man in the bathroom mirror, who had aged ten years in the last eighteen months, and realised I needed a holiday, a break from the investigations, the quarrels, and the memories of a man—*a friend*—who'd died because of secrets.

Those were my secrets as well; I shared some, buried others. I'd opened up to my superiors, who accepted my resignation, and for the first time since I was a teenage boy, long before my sister drowned, I felt free, alive. No responsibilities; no threats to my life. The only black fly in the Mediterranean sand had been my father, still able to exert influence in police matters on Malta. His name and memory carried weight amongst friends, and there were many who remained loyal to the man.

Thus, after three months of spending my time knee-deep in remorse, drinking my way around the island and fending off enquiries into my health, I was summoned by the new chief and 'asked' to look into the death of a well-known journalist and activist. It was made clear why I had been chosen to join the team, but it still rankled with me that I was given no choice but to agree to the job.

I avoided old areas for a while, preferring to live a life that was ready to spiral down the toilet in the beautiful surroundings of Mellieha. I kept away from Valetta, I started seeing less of friends—the only person I was in contact with during that time was Aakster, my Dutch Magpie.

I still got a phone call every few days. The bond forged while we erased a cancer that threatened to suffocate Europe—in the tunnels that once housed a frightened populace during the dark days of World War Two, no less—forever entangled us, it seemed. I just wished she were here. I wished I could see her. I should have been grateful to hear her voice, that accent, her laugh. Indeed, I could have done with her advice when I was cajoled back into working for the island's police force. Instead, I had to listen to righteous platitudes, promises that it would be different this time: the bad apples I had helped uncover were no longer in a position to see the public's charge of corruption hold sway.

I stared hard into the eyes of my reflection and tormentor, the sound of my youth playing in the bedroom as Steve Rothery's guitar solo kicked in. I allowed my mind to focus on the day on which it changed. So many of them, so many divergent paths that could have been taken, but it is that day—the one when I took the phone call informing me of my friend's mother's death— which occupied my thoughts. I was sure my eyes went blank with the pain.

Losing one's mind is a terrible thing. I saw my parents traverse a similar route when my sister drowned trying to impress a young boy. I felt the first snag of my own barely contained threads come loose when I was taken in by evil—when I found my ex-wife had died at the hands of that same diseased mind. And then, as we stood on the cliff and let my friend's ashes find their way to peace, I heard them strain and become looser still.

How Aakster survived her own demons during that brief period I never found out, but then, she'd lived with demons all her life and hers far surpassed my own.

I don't think I helped with the inquiry into the death of the journalist. I felt as though I was only brought on board to calm a politically volatile situation, and whilst I have no truck with any politician of any persuasion, knowing my duty was merely to keep order…I felt dirty. I started drinking harder to numb the pain.

The pain increased when I was 'requested' to re-join on a full-time basis, to take up the position of detective once more. "It is what the public wants," I was told, and, thanks to my father's name, I had to accept, once more stepping into the shadow of a man who could not see me for anything other than the boy who nearly destroyed all he had worked for. I had sympathy now for the damaged; my dead eyes saw nothing worth living for.

Another guitar solo, a line about Kerouac—*does everything have to remind me of my friend?* The day after Aakster had departed for Holland, I took a bus out to St. Julian's Bay and sat in wonder as one of my friend's favourite modern poets, the one he called the Maltese Songbird, performed her latest works to an audience lapping up the romance of the evening sun as it danced its nightly tango off the glasses in the Seabreeze Restaurant. For a while, I was content. Not happy; melancholy blues wrapped in traumatised disorientation. I clapped out of love for words I felt privileged to hear, but my attention was continually drawn to the steep hill that contained Triq Scicluna and the first line of a poem that conveyed the anger and sadness of a stoned poet's finest work.

I made my excuses to my host, thanking her once again for a superb evening—even gave my appreciation to the chef for a meal that was nothing short of exceptional, despite my barely managing to eat the fish I had ordered—and made my way up to the side street that ran between Our Lady of Mount Carmel and the sharp corner that hugged the delicate bay. The short walk seemed to take forever, a sluggish trail that shone in the shadow of yet another dying sun. Finally, as the distance between footfalls shortened, I looked up from the bottom of the hill and read the words once more and knew that this fleeting sentence was not meant for his time, but our own. Madness begets madness and suffering is the mother of death.

Enough. Time to shave, to capture a smile of responsibility on my face and turn the record over. Breakfast called: Mellieħa had a few places where they would find me a corner into which I could crawl for a while and avoid the calls, play out the time until either I accepted my part in a man's death or joined him— a pair of phantoms holding court next to Oliver Reed's shrine in the capital.

The phone rang. Typical really, a semblance of a plan having formed, a diversion to Debbie's and the allure of the broken dreams afforded by a glass of wine before nine in the morning. Putting down my shaving brush, I left the bathroom behind and walked into the bedroom, turning down the volume on the record player as I picked up the phone, feeling more than a little disappointed that the number shown was not of my Magpie.

Do you ever look at a number on your phone's display screen and wonder who the hell it is? First instinct is to dismiss it completely, to press end even before the conversation has started. I did that. An international number—no, thanks. Not going to go down that particular rabbit hole. You never know what box of crazy you are about to open.

I threw the phone down on the bed and wished to hell I could join it, grovel between the sheets and put a pillow over my head. Sometimes when the dark had been too much, I fantasised about someone doing it for me, tightly. I wouldn't struggle, a sweet release.

I turned over the record to its B-side, twisted the volume control beyond what had been playing and then resumed the act of shaving, ignoring the phone as it rang a second and third time over the following ten minutes. When, finally, I was sure I looked as decent as I could without having some young graduate from human resources offer a chair and watch me go through personal agony as they ask me to relate how I feel, all the time finding novel ways to angle their head and nod gently and empathise, I went back to the bed and picked up the phone. Same number, no name—looked like the country code for America. I didn't know anyone in America. Must've been a mistake.

It was on the fourth attempt that I let curiosity win the day and answered in my official tone, allowing the speaker to confirm that it was me he wanted. He introduced himself and asked if I was able to help in a case he was working on. Did I know a Doctor Corrish who worked at the university? I replied in the negative, not wishing to divulge that I had purposely stayed away from the faculty since my friend died, away from the halls and rooms where we had caught up on local gossip as the smell of teenage rebellion and twenty-something resignation drowned out the bouquet of learning. The world didn't care if you were unique, only that you had ways to pay your bills, and I didn't want to become part of a system with its own rules and agendas.

I sat at my desk—an easy task as I only had enough space in my apartment for the essentials these days, no longer willing to keep a home that was only used for showing the world how important I was—and began taking notes.

My caller was a police captain from Cleveland, a man who talked straight but with anger for a system he had once been proud of and that still beat hard within him. He kept his request short, and it was a reasonable one, but one which should have gone through official channels. I sensed someone else was holding the leash; an old dog commanded to bark did not do so willingly; it did so to avoid a beating from a cruel owner. I had known the type before, tough and fearless but, having been shown a way out of the monotony their life had become, prepared to follow orders one final time.

He assured me the official line would be drawn; the order came from the main opposition running for office in Cleveland—a woman in whom the city and surrounding area had placed their political hopes.

He asked if I was aware of the Samantha Ó Foghladh case from 1992—the disappearance of a young woman who had left home and never returned. Again, I replied in the negative. I had been but a young man at that time. Over the course of the next ten minutes, Captain Holt imparted the case history—last seen buying a ticket in Pittsburgh, overheard saying she was on her way to Paris to join her sister but never arrived—and what had come to light in the past few days: a revelation in the form of two letters: one to the newspapers and one to the home address of the missing woman.

It is always a shock when new evidence is presented long after the trail goes cold. Sometimes it comes with more than a big swift kick of suspicion. However, I reminded Holt that I had no arrest warrant for Doctor Corrish.

"All taken care of," he muttered somewhat sharply as if I were being lured into a carefully sprung trap. "By the time you get to the university, your superiors will have all the necessary documents. It's being treated as murder. Diplomatically sensitive."

I could not help myself; after all, the chain of command had somewhat been compromised. "How did you get my number?" I asked. I had not long changed it.

"From a mutual friend, Aakster…"

At the revelation my Magpie was his cousin's daughter, a smile crept over my face for the first time in nearly two years. She'd always said the links between us all were more than circumstantial. Everybody knew everybody, it seemed…and yet I didn't know Doctor Corrish, nor did I know why a prospective political leader was asking for this man to be arrested.

The first point didn't matter for now. The second one bothered me, though, and I asked Holt who she was. His answer hit me hard. It shouldn't have done, I guess; in a world of connections, it is the ones we don't expect which are the most relatable. She was the missing woman's sister.

Five years older than Samantha, she had left home in the summer of 1987, determined to find a way to improve her life and get away from their violent father, her regret that she couldn't take her sister buried deep until she was able to send the money for Samantha to join her in Paris. Holt suggested her regret may be masking guilt—"After all," he said softly, "it was well known Raymond Ó Foghladh was handy with his fists, spending many a night in the lock-up, always ready with the apologies the next day." There was also the allegation that sometime after his wife died he had forced himself on his youngest daughter—something he and the middle child, a boy, had angrily denied and was later found to be false.

Was it from this environment that the young woman had run, unable to deal with the disease festering within the home, the smell of closeted, possible rape, the fear of being alone? Not for the first time, I thought of my ex-wife, of her loneliness, her need for constant attention. When she didn't get it, she would make eyes at another, always concerned with her own satisfaction. Not the same. Choices made; different paths taken.

All information imparted, I thanked Holt and phoned the commissar to ask if he had received the official paperwork. Receiving an affirmative, I called through to Headquarters and asked the duty officer if he would send a constable to pick me up and then drive me to the university to arrest Doctor Corrish. I put on a tie, a sober one, black—my unconscious reminding me I was stepping into an arena where I did not wish to fight. There would be students there who had known my friend, as well as those who only knew the rumours of the spectre that once filled the corridors with his knowledge of language and personality that was captivating and dangerous in equal measure.

I mused on the idea written by a stranger that ghosts are just unfinished business. I forget who typed the words, but in this case, it held true. I was walking back into the light, armed only with phantoms to guide me in taking down a man who had allegedly taunted the Cleveland police and the family of a missing woman nearly thirty years after she was last seen.

I always believed that before your death, in that final moment when life holds on for the eternal, all your sins call on you and give you reason to make amends. I saw it in the last days of my friend, the acknowledgement of his role in our downfall, his notebook confirming his double life. Was this out of guilt—the desperation to annul the pain promised him by his own ghost?

Is this what had happened to Doctor Corrish? Some devastating news that made him believe he too had to offer his soul up for redemption?

I am not a religious man. Too much has happened in my life to see in such absolutes, and a small part of my heart went out to Corrish—guilty of murder, perhaps, but is it only the fanatical and hate-filled who renew the suffering of a family that has learned to live with its grief? I don't think so. I think the repentant also try to reach out beyond the lonely grave they dug for themselves so long ago.

The constable turned up within the half hour. As we drove to the university, I started to read the man's file.

Chapter Three

A False Trail

Part of a Missing Woman's Journal, 1992

H E WAS NICE, perhaps the first nice boy I had met in a long time, the kind of boy who you knew liked you, but who would forever stay silent, suffering almost in his tongue-tied appreciation, reserved but willing to talk about any number of subjects. A nice boy; a good man; and I hated lying to him.

I smiled at him as he got on the bus, a coy temptation to have someone remember me, to take note of my life as I sought a way to leave it behind. We talked from Cleveland all the way to Pittsburgh, our coats dragged over our knees to protect our mutual modesty, our conversation open and richly fulfilling. I finally got to know someone other than a family member or a school friend, though there were few of those whom I saw outside of class, thanks to my father's overpowering, dominating presence.

Truth be told, I had noticed him before he made his way to the bus. Travelling alone with a large, cumbersome and surely back-aching rucksack, he walked with his head bowed, staring at his shoes, scuffed and worn down by the road he had taken—a short trip to clear his head of the pressures of home, he told me later. His family expected him to follow in the footsteps of his older sister, who had done well at university and of whom everybody was justifiably proud. He felt he could not live up to their expectations, their desire for him to be something he wasn't. I saw that in him; he was different—none of the stomach-churning, sickening, frightening arrogance I had seen in many other boys and men.

I watched him—studied would be a more accurate description—for an hour, yet he didn't notice me. We sat there without saying a word to each other, surrounded by late-night travellers—the group of Amish women who sat upright, projecting an air of prominence and care as they made devout small talk and deferred their reverence to a grey-haired older gentleman dressed head to toe in coal-dirt, broad-fall trousers and what seemed to my eyes a mourning jacket. The beard worn by—I'd thought—all Amish men was strangely missing. Perhaps his thin, gaunt face could not have worn the excess hair without making the old man stumble under the weight of experience and pride. His jacket was slightly open at the top, as if he wanted to reveal his soul but not his heart, and beneath the coat a white shirt of plain belief, unadorned by the symbols of the age whereby everybody became a billboard, willing to brand themselves in some sort of unholy deal with a fashion-conscious devil while paying for the pleasure of being seen as hip.

The boy caught my eye for the same reason. A plain black cap—an item of function rather than style—sat comfortably on his head; his plain white T-shirt bore no signals to passion or orientation, no signposts of need or humour; his plain black jeans looked a size too big for him and were held up by plain black suspenders that sat tightly against his frame. The only colour to be seen was the orange felt that covered his ears as he listened to his Walkman and gently hummed along, avoiding eye contact or ignoring all that he didn't want to see. Plain, unobtrusive, projecting tiredness, a boy no one would remember but who, in this late addition to the plan, would remember me.

I don't know why that mattered. As the prospect of my journey began to overwhelm me, I somehow grasped onto the notion that I needed to be remembered, that at least one kind person might think of me in this corner of the States far away from the anger that had dominated my life since Mom died and you, my sister, moved away.

You warned me: *Speak to no one. The bastard doesn't deserve to know why you left—he won't even care—but should he report it then the questions will start, and he will feel some of the heat that he inflicted upon us returned to him. Let him starve under the gaze of public appeal. Let him feel as if he is drowning and then understand what it means to hide away from the accusations and stares. Then, in time, we will present you in Paris with me—a story made better. You will be with me.*

I lied to the boy. Not everything, of course. I enjoyed his company, though he was a little stoned, certainly tired, having travelled from Hamilton in Canada that morning. Before that, he'd spent almost a month hanging out in an abandoned property near Cedar Point. I don't think he wanted to leave; he just wanted to share some history with his grandfather who came from there but who died before he was born, fighting for freedom on a beach, leaving a grieving woman to bring up the boy's father alone.

I nearly didn't stay on the bus as it wound its way to Philadelphia. I almost went with him to whatever deserted highway lay beyond that stop he said was his last. How that would have ended I don't know. Probably terribly, but I would have relished the chance to get to know him better, to save him, for I believed he was on a course to self-destruction. Maybe not then, as he contemplated slipping into the light of motel darkness and wondering if the company he shared his bed with for the night would bite and leave future tales and medical bills as a fond farewell in the morning.

It's funny to think of me wanting to make sure someone was all right, especially after the lies I told him during our journey together. White lies. I said I was going to study art in Paris, when I hadn't known what I would do as I slipped into my new life. I did promise I would write him, though. He gave me a home address in England; he would be there soon enough. I think he just wanted to know that I was OK. I will honour that.

He asked me to call him Ash, wouldn't tell me his last name, said that didn't matter, and I believed him, this strange silent boy.

I said I nearly stayed with him as we went our separate ways. Twice more I thought about getting off the bus along the way to Philadelphia; twice more I found myself forcing down temptation like I had never done before. After all, I saw which motel he went into; he was tired so he wouldn't have gotten too far in the next couple of days. But like all temptation, you have to swallow the urge to act, refuse to give in to the demands of a fledgling heart. Sex was not what I wanted—too much of that had already happened. He hadn't offered that anyway, though we'd talked with a degree of intimacy while the other passengers drifted in and out of sleep, nudged awake by the occasional pothole or the sound of a crying baby groping for its mother's tit and being swatted away as easily as an irritating fly circling meat laid out for that evening's feast. Occasionally, the ladies in black mumbled a silent prayer of devotion, and the beardless gaunt man wrote a sermon.

We became friends. *Friends.* If I were his friend, I would have told him the truth, the reason why I rode a bus in the middle of the night. I would have made him my private confessor—forgive me, Father, for I have sinned. I have lied and not been true to the past. Forgive me, Father, please pray with me, let this sinner repent, for I think I may have killed my father. I hit him so hard he will surely bleed out across the ravages of worn-down floorboards, consoled only by the beetles and rats that will tear at his flesh.

Could I tell him that, this stoned boy who needs not a conscious to absolve but a heart to mend?

Best to lie, to tell a story. He won't remember much anyway—just enough that if I am stopped along the way then someone will think kindly of me, for as I write this, I cannot look at myself with any degree of sympathy or love.

I told him my name and stretched out my hand in welcome, making sure he would not sit anywhere but next to me. He offered me a cigarette and apologised when I pointed out the peeling sticker on the window rebuking such actions. In truth, I would have gladly taken a couple and smoked them along the way—I would even have cheerfully snogged the boy in payment, but that was a deal I used to have, just to be close to someone who wouldn't hurt me.

I told him my real name. I could have lied about that, but I wanted a connection, something to stir the memory if anything should go wrong with the plan. The way I'd left my father on the kitchen floor, I pretty much figured the plan had gone awry.

About half an hour into the journey, he started to cry, and I instinctively reached out and took his hand. He didn't fight it. I don't think he even registered my small act of compassion. His voice wavered as he spoke of having travelled so far yet never wanting to stop, to keep going and never return to the mental torture that still ate away at his mind. He was lost in a country that wasn't his, and the return to nature he had sought, in truth, had left him feeling humiliated by his unwillingness to sever the ties that bound him to expectation and demand.

I had found a kindred spirit, a couple of years older than me, just as world-weary, just as sentimental about the way the past hindered the future and our responses to it, but also one well versed in music. He told me he had been listening to a collection of songs he had recorded over several months before his flight across a star-filled sky, an ocean that roared in hunger below. He showed me some of the tapes; I was impressed by the designs on the front, which he shyly told me he had drawn, the handwriting delicate, almost feminine, and the inlay cards explaining their significance. This was his travel journal—a list of names and places beside each track. There was a tape dedicated solely to the likes of David Bowie, Supertramp, Marillion, Genesis, Metallica and Bruce Springsteen, and odd collections which didn't seem to fit together but, when viewed from his point of view, connected his life and the journey he had taken.

I asked what he had been listening to as he boarded the bus, when he saw me smile and removed his earphones. He opened up the imitation-metal opening of the Walkman and showed me a possession of gold: the *Nevermind* album by Nirvana. It was one I had also come to love, albeit not being able to own a copy myself as my father would not let me have such music in the house. I found myself nodding wildly in glee when Ash asked if I wanted to listen, and hand in hand, sometimes asking a question, other moments spent in reflection, we drove across highways in our minds and chased the moon until it dipped in the shadow of the looming glass giants that made up the city in the distance.

I was glad to have made a connection with someone, not just to give me an alibi later should I need one, but because in amongst my anger and bitterness at the thoughtless, undesired caress life had shoved against my body, I had found someone who was just that nice.

We parted, I promised to write, I didn't know if he would return the favour, but I hoped he would, and as I watched from behind the dusky window and the sticker proclaiming the penalty for smoking that I had been absent-mindedly picking at for several hours, he crossed the road and headed to the nearest motel. The weight of the world briefly removed from his shoulders now pulled down on his spine, making him seem older, as damaged as he had been when I first saw him looking down to hell as if he were pleading for them to take him in.

Nearing Philadelphia, there were very few souls on the bus. It had been lonely and dull, but there on the road, I felt the safest I had been for many years. I had the memory of a boy named Ash to keep me going. Not long until I changed for New York—I was glad I took that route rather than going up to Buffalo and downstate to the big city or else I would never have met him. I might even have headed home, owned up to striking back at my father and then spent the rest of my life in jail.

Should I call the house to make sure he is all right? Call a neighbour perhaps, tell them I've gone out of town for a few days and haven't heard from him?

There were always home invasions around our neighbourhood, always the chance that a housebreaker would find the back door unlocked. Always a chance that our father, having fallen asleep under the influence of a few late-afternoon beers, might have met his end at the hand of one who didn't know how dirt poor we were, that the drunken fuck had sold everything valuable to kick back at—as he perceived it—the injustice of the world.

Bastard, bastard, bastard. I hate him. I hope he is dead, but that means there is a mess for you to clean up. Your clean, spacious life in your clean, spacious apartment will be turned upside down, dragged through the mire of my making.

I wonder. If I told you all I have written over the years, would you step forward and tell the truth about how you left me there in that sinkhole to fend off his advances, to be his slave, a whore for others to paw at. You will never understand. I love you, my dear sister, but you never listened, and while I may have told Ash a series of lies just to keep the casual conversation ticking over, to embed me into his mind, I know he cared deeply.

That one kiss, sweet and savoured, a hand held as he cried for a future he could not avoid—it was real to Ash, that strange, lost boy pining for a life of solitude and thought. I could see that even if he couldn't; that is all I needed to know. But the real reason I knew it was real, why the time spent in his company meant a great deal to me too, was his leaving present.

A small exchange of gifts: I had given him my time and compassion, but what he gave me in return was far greater. It was a piece of him. After the bus drove away into the night, I went into my coat pocket to get a tissue only to find that he had, discreetly and with obvious affection, placed the album we had listened to inside—a neatly written *Thank you, Samantha* in the margins of his artwork, "Come As You Are" just below it.

I cried. If I could have howled without disturbing those few hardy travellers—those who liked the long, exhausting trip, the ones who had no other way to get from point A to B without going through their own version of slumming in hell and the toilet spillage that crept under the door—then I would have done so.

In a world full of shits, occasionally you find a rose willing to face the storm. I held on to that tape. I had nothing to play it on, but I could hear every song perfectly.

Chapter Four

Finally, I've Got My Man

The Ohio Captain

I KNEW Ó FOGHLADH, a bastard of a man. I knew his daughter too—the one whose disappearance and obvious murder I had been assigned to investigate in '92. Although no body was ever found, I knew in my gut that she was dead, and over planned coffee meetings that my wife knew about and some late-night whiskey at functions that she didn't, I had gotten to know the older daughter as well. Ó Foghladh, though, he was a tough nut, what they once would have called a *man's man*. I just called him a two-bit asshole—it's a wonder he wasn't killed a lot earlier.

I hadn't expected Catherine Ó Foghladh to reach out to me in 2016 and tell me she was thinking about running for office. A big name since she'd returned soon after the events of September 11, she'd funded a few projects with her backers, by way of thanking a city she said had never forgotten losing one of its own. How true that was I didn't know, but it had the effect she sought, and she became a hero to many in Cleveland, a beacon of hope that others clung to, and she welcomed it.

I come out here occasionally, onto the streets of my city, to think and escape, too long strapped in a chair I didn't want, with paperwork coming out of my ears and a constant nagging pain in my lower back. The streets were always mine; I was a young cop right here. I did what was needed and I made mistakes, but I learned from it; I grew. But that night when Dispatch called out over the radio that a murder had taken place at an address many of us recognised, my blood ran cold.

I didn't have much to do with Ó Foghladh. There are criminals and there are bastards, and he was certainly very much in the latter camp—a mean drunk who ran errands for some shady characters. I always suspected he liked his daughter a little too much. The bruises on her face that she maintained were the result of school bullying, I was sure came from him when she wouldn't give in to his demands. But I could never question him; I could never arrest the son of a bitch. He was always protected; someone kept the good guys from delving deeper into his life, and God knows I tried. It stopped me from reaching the position I tenuously hold now, at least a decade later than I would have liked and beyond which I will not advance because of my suspicions.

A couple of other, more senior detectives had arrived at the scene before me, almost as if they had been around the corner, eyeing up the talent in the bar at the end of the block, but that was none of my business. I had only been in the job a year, and some apples you don't look at when you bite down on them. They soon cleared out, their contention that it was a burglary gone too far and we'd catch the guy soon enough, and that was it. They asked if I wanted to join them for a beer. I said no, and they waved me off with little concern.

Hanging around that scene was an experience. I had witnessed the aftereffects of gang-related violence. I had seen knives sticking out of overweight bellies, too many to count rape victims, drugs and junkies by the bucket load—if I was lucky I got to see some of them clean. In 1980s inner-city Cleveland, the American dream had soured, and so had the poison they were pushing into every available vein and opening.

For all of that, I had never seen anything like that murder scene. His eyes appeared as if they were shooting steel laser beams, a small blade sticking out of each one, and his tongue was half-severed, flopping idly out of one side of his mouth. Flies gathered in and around the small, open wound in his head—he appeared to have been hit with something sharp. His hands had been tied behind his back, and both thumbs, like his tongue, hung by a thread of sinew. I didn't care to look and see what else might have been severed and ultimately had no need: the first-on-scene local officer had already found the missing appendage tossed in the fireplace on the other side of the room. Burglary gone wrong my ass. It was not my call, though I could have said something. To my shame, I turned a blind eye; after all, the neighbourhood was better off without this depraved man on its streets.

What was important to me was Samantha. Had she been subjected to the same barbarism, the brutality? She wasn't anywhere in the building, and house-to-house visits brought the same answer: she had been seen leaving the house with a small bag over her shoulder about a week before, but no sighting since. Many assumed she had finally had enough and just gone, skipped town, but she would be back as soon as she heard the news.

I had known Samantha for about five years. Trouble, I thought, but a sweet kid she turned out to be. I caught her one day, shoplifting candy from a store not far from her home. I was in the back of the premises visiting the owner's mother, who had supplied a character reference for a woman I wanted to be our cleaner. At the time, my wife was still grieving over the death of our unborn child, and with my job taking up so much of my time, I wanted to take the pressure off her—and also stay out of her way if possible. I knew no different; it was another era. I would handle it better now.

So I caught Samantha stealing, but to my surprise, the owner didn't want to prosecute her. She was just a kid, he said, and besides, she was the daughter of Raymond Ó Foghladh. No further explanation needed: I understood why he didn't want to hang her out to dry. Raymond Ó Foghladh, sick bastard that he was, would have found a way to be home on the very night that the shop was firebombed. A man of Irish temper, to whom the war was not over, made many an enemy regret standing up to him.

I asked Samantha when she had last eaten. She shrugged, and I guessed it had been at least a couple of days. She looked sick, white with pain and stick-thin. Children and Family Services should have been involved, but some people don't want to be helped. I told the owner I would deal with Samantha and took her for some food. I got through to that kid in a way I could never have done with the child my wife and I lost, but I was also worried for her safety. She wouldn't leave her father; family loyalty was always the driving force in sad cases like this.

I didn't find out where she had last been seen until a couple of nights later, when a woman who worked at the Greyhound bus station said she recognised the girl from the local news. She had sold Samantha a ticket to Pittsburgh about a week before. I cannot adequately describe the sense of jubilation this news brought me, for it confirmed she could not have been party to her father's demise, despite her fingerprints being on the ornament that had on it samples of the dead man's blood and hair.

The apologies I received from the bus station owners when I asked if there were any cameras in the area were off the scale. No recordings anywhere that night due to a routine maintenance overhaul—I admit I let my temper get the better of me, and I was suspended from the case. But I didn't let it go. Some leads came my way, and I checked them out: I contacted the managers in Pittsburgh the day after and was told that no young single woman had got off the bus there, only a crowd of Amish, a couple of older black gentlemen, a young white man with a backpack and a couple of ladies carrying children.

I even spoke to the driver—a helpful fellow who confirmed what his bosses had said. He didn't even remember a young woman being on the bus. Could she have stayed on, gone further into the depths of the unknown? His answer, like many others, was disappointing. He checked the bus at Philadelphia, where his night ended, and there was nobody left on board. Where she had gotten to, how she had evaded the driver, I still don't know, but I have my theories.

I concentrated on the boy. The driver told me he was listening to music when he got on and waved at the bus when he left—"An odd thing to do, eccentric, probably stoned. I smelled something funny about him when he got on, but hey, live and let live, and as long as he stayed quiet… That time of night, I don't need the hassle."

The driver did remember something, though: he thought he saw something on the boy's pants—blood, maybe—something that reflected in the orange streetlight as a couple of kids on bikes took to the streets in competition. "I nearly called him back," he told me, "but he was gone. Crossed the street and only looking back to wave." The driver couldn't describe the boy, and I had the bus impounded, but it had been cleaned to within a whisker of its life. I had nothing but empty suspicions and a missing girl.

I pressed my captain into looking at her father's murder with less cynical eyes or perhaps those not in the pay of someone else. For that, I nearly lost my job altogether, yet it soon came to light that Ó Foghladh's murder was a hit, not a burglary gone wrong nor the woman of the house finally exacting her revenge. But time moves on; nobody was arrested; nobody missed the father, not even the sister, our hoped-to-be new civic and political leader. Nobody even missed Samantha, time moves on, but for me, I never forgot.

Then just a couple of weeks back, something strange landed on my desk—a note to contact a fellow officer in New Jersey. I called the number. The officer, a desk sergeant no doubt with a waistline to match his experience, said he could be wrong— "Records get lost over the years, transfer of buildings, obscene waste in management, paperwork, you know the story"—but he remembered a young man who'd outstayed his visa, a British kid. Luckily, he'd made his own notes at the time and proudly informed me the kid's name was Ash Corrish. I asked why he'd waited so long to pass on the information, the case was nearly thirty years old. He couldn't give me an answer.

I put my suspicions to Catherine Ó Foghladh the next day over breakfast. I told her about the call and my quick fact-checking on Corrish, who was no longer in Britain, but he was still alive. Her face…well, the shock turned her white, as if the lost decades had been too much for her to take. We discussed our next move. It was going to be difficult without proof; after all, Samantha was missing, not officially dead, even though Catherine had privately confided to me a couple of years earlier that she knew deep down her sister was dead. I'd told her then, as I told her that morning, to keep heart, stay strong, and in an instant she composed herself.

She asked where the man lived now, and I told her he was some sort of teacher in Malta. The blood rushed back to her face, and I thought she was going to explode in a mass of fury and fly there immediately, hell-bent on revenge. Instead, it was with a calm flush of newfound lust that she came up with a plan. She knew a detective in Malta—not personally but by reputation—who had brought down a violent drug lord. She was sure we could get him to arrest Corrish, quickly sort out the paperwork and bring him to America for questioning.

I didn't think her plan was feasible and told her as much. We had no proof, just a name remembered decades after the fact. However, she persisted, excited by the possible lead and almost sweating as she raised her voice to the point where others around us took notice.

"I finally have my man!" she exclaimed over and over again, punching the air unconscious. She became animated, telling me she would work out the details and get in touch with the relevant bodies to start the ball rolling. I, on the other hand, was to make contact with this detective on Malta and get him to arrest Corrish.

"I don't know him," I argued, but she played on my darkest regret, reminding me that we had both let down her sister—and her father.

"Surely this boy had something to do with Samantha's disappearance! He might even have been responsible for our father's death too. Have you thought about that? What a crowning glory it would be for a man coming to the end of a wonderful career!"

She finished off by alluding to the possibility of it leading to better things, working alongside her in office, and I sat there and nodded, not comfortable but wanting this chapter of my life to close—one that had seen me take the fall for others' negligence.

"I am going to forward you a name," she said. "This woman is a friend of the island detective. If he plays dumb or sticks to procedure…I dunno, drop into the request that you are her cousin. He'll believe it. Once the deed is done, we can backtrack and say he misheard."

With that, she gathered her things and stood to her full height, her crisp white skirt and blouse catching the rays of yet another fine Cleveland morning. She bent to kiss my cheek, whispering, "You've sacrificed so much—it's time to reap the rewards of all your efforts."

Something didn't feel right as I called the waiter over to order another cup of coffee and ask for the check, which Catherine had forgotten to pay in her excitement. There was a nagging feeling, one that went back to the night we discovered Raymond Ó Foghladh's body. Samantha had skipped town a week before; we had dismissed her as a suspect on those grounds many years ago, so how could the boy be involved?

I took out the picture of Corrish I'd found on the internet; it was taken at a seminar and printed in one of the British national newspapers. Corrish was slight, perhaps capable of murdering a young woman, but not a two-hundred-pound man with a temper as large as his girth. He'd have chewed Corrish to pieces.

But then I replayed Catherine's words and felt the adrenaline surge through me. *My final case, time to reap the rewards.* Like Catherine, I finally had my man, and I felt good about it.

I could see the headlines flash before me and allowed them to feed my ego—a false sign of the self-worth I had countless times instructed recruits and young detectives to dismiss. Their place was on the team; this was a den in which no individual could thrive alone. Yet there I was, dreaming of finishing my career with the bust that had eluded the top brass all those years ago.

Coffee at any time of day is good. It courses through the mind and allows you to believe you have the world at your feet. That is when it is at its most potent, and I was awake at last. The backwater of Europe was no match for America's finest. I would call this detective, and I would spin him the lie. For how long he'd buy it, I didn't know, but Catherine was confident it would take him a while to figure it out, and by then, the boy—the man known as Ash Corrish—would be in our hands and telling all he knew.

I finally had my man.

Chapter Five

Nobody's Errand Boy

The Detective

READING A PERSON'S file leaves me wondering about the nature of disconnection. You only see what someone else wants you to see, and unless you do your own investigation, dig around at the stuff pencilled in the fringes, then you are certainly doing someone else's dirty work. *Always question.* It was a lesson I learned late in life.

Ashkii Corrish: the photograph attached to the folder by a solitary paperclip doesn't do the name justice. It is… exotic, a name that inspires confidence. I looked through the window of the door that locked him away from the rest of the world; I couldn't be sure if he was asleep or just concentrating, but then I saw the slight fidget of his fingers, the tapping of each one in turn from left to right, from the little finger across the two thumbs and onto the farthest finger on his right hand, a moment's pause and then back again. It had to be some sort of coping mechanism, a way to fend off the dragon in his mind and stop panic from overwhelming him. I was sure I had heard of this before, this ritual of anxiety.

He was a plain-looking man, certainly no film star, though perhaps an extra—the background waiter hovering at the elbow of the doomed woman as she orders her final meal before succumbing to the bullet delivered by the assassin poised on a distant rooftop, her lipstick smudging as the blood trickled from her mouth, alluring and deadly. Despite his unremarkable looks, I imagined, though this was not always the case, that Corrish had broken a couple of hearts in his youth. Was this girl Samantha one of them? Life had been unfair to this man, and as I watched through the small window, half-hidden in shadow, I had the feeling that for all the bluster that came down the telephone from the Ohio captain, this was not the man they wanted. Call it intuition, call it a hunch, but this man was too feeble, too awkward to carry off the crime of which those across the Atlantic had accused him.

Of course, looks can deceive, and until I went through that door and started interviewing him, I could not be certain of my suspicion. His sparse file gave little away: one black stain, and was it really that big a deal when examined under the duress of youthful exploration? Deported from the United States after outstaying his six-month visa, not a single parking ticket, but there was a gap and not just his undocumented stay in the States, but a period of a year in which he seemed to have been completely off the grid. I worked out the timeline: if he'd been sent back home at twenty-one, then completed three years of university, between the ages of twenty-four and twenty-five he was essentially missing, or perhaps just overlooked by the system.

Two living relatives, a mother and an older sister, residing in Oxfordshire.

A second-class degree from Birmingham, a year's gap and then a distinction from the Open University. Why had he not continued straight away? If he'd taken time out from finishing college to go travelling, why take another year out? Where had he been?

There was a phone number for his sister; I made a mental note to call her after the interview.

I opened the door, fully expecting him to come out of his trance-like state and face me, but I don't think he heard me enter the room. His fingers kept tapping and his eyes remained closed. I moved slowly towards the table, my gaze fixed upon his movements. It wasn't until the young police officer slammed the door—with such a force that I communicated him a silent, stony-faced rebuke—that Ashkii Corrish opened his eyes with a snap. He looked as if he was about to let go of his dignity in a manner unbecoming of him.

I smiled kindly; I was not here to play games. I had a job to do, of course, but since my friend died, since the events in the tunnels that once housed creatures hiding from bombs, I had seen that nothing came of conveying menace to someone who was already frightened. I knew instinctively that he was going to spill his guts, whether he was guilty or not. He would tell the truth; he had that look about him, wide-eyed and terrified.

There was a knock at the door, and I bade them enter. His court-appointed lawyer appeared, made his apologies and sat next to his client. Now there was a man with guilt written all over his face. I would rather have interrogated him on his whereabouts the last couple of hours. He was young, fresh-faced and olive-skinned from too many evenings soaking up the sun somewhere on the island, no doubt rubbing oil into thighs and nibbling down on the fruit of his labours.

I returned my attention to the man across from me and turned on the recorder. After the formalities, I asked him his name for clarification. The first hint of apology came as he answered but then added, "Just Ash is all right." He caught my brief quizzical look and offered the explanation that it had been a long time since anyone had called him Ashkii, a hangover from his grandmother badgering his father to name him after his grandfather, who had died during World War Two—"I prefer Ash. My mother still calls me Ashkii when I telephone her…I don't think she remembers. Alzheimer's can be very cruel."

I nodded in understanding, having long since realised the name we call ourselves is a promise that we are not the children of memory but the forgivers of the future; we shape the world in which we hear our name spoken.

"Your grandfather," I said, "I guess he was not English?"

A brief smile of recognition filtered across his greyish-tinged lips. I studied him closely. His eyes, perhaps once a dark, brilliant blue, had faded. An early sign of cataracts maybe, but he didn't wear glasses, at least, not in here and not when we arrested him at the university. He was tall but not excessively so, his hair lank—the Maltese sun had done him no favours in that department—and I acknowledged he was dark of complexion rather than tanned as I'd first suspected.

He smiled as he spoke, only deferring to sadness once when he finished. His grandfather had been Canadian—"A 'half-breed' he always said. British mother, Navajo father. His name wasn't even Ashkii, it was William, but he was called it when he was in my great-grandmother's good books. It means boy. He never knew his father—a sense of symmetry that seems to dog our family history. My great-grandmother met him when she was helping out on a research project, human instinct took its course, and three months after she returned to England, she gave birth to my grandfather.

"He returned to Canada to search for his father in 1938, but he had moved on, a nomad who should never have left his tribe in search of something else. My grandfather stayed for a while but came home when war broke out. He met my grandmother and the rest is history. I am the result of conversation and intrigue. I bear his name…I just don't like the long form much."

I nodded. He had been forthcoming about the details of his life so far, and I could detect no ruse in his voice to suggest that he was lying.

He then pulled me out of my observation by asking, "How did she die?"

I detected a shift in position from the young constable. He too had been staring hard at the man opposite us. It was a strange question to ask, and for a while, I didn't answer. I watched the analogue clock over the door tick around a full, deserted, silent minute. I wanted to know why he thought she was dead. Sad eyes seemed to want to confess something. It wasn't a normal reaction—a normal question—yet I still had no sense of him trying to lead us down a dirt path of misdirection.

Despite the Ohio police captain's insistence that this was a murder case, I could see only that it was a missing person inquiry. Yes, missing person investigations on occasion led to a murder case being opened, but some people don't want to be found. It doesn't mean they have died at the hands of a stranger.

I stalled Corrish, returning to the subject of his grandfather. He sighed, not out of exasperation, out of tiredness. I realised then that he had been carrying around this thought for all his life. Where once it may have been a heavy burden, now it was killing him.

Over the next half an hour, and without interruption, he told us all that we needed to know. He'd arrived in New York, worked for a while in one of the kitchens, waited on the occasional table and run errands for the guests, keeping his nose clean, keeping out of trouble, just happy to be away from home. After a few months, he had saved up enough to head north, first stopping in Rochester, then on to Buffalo and the United States side of Niagara Falls. Finally, he'd made the choice to go into Canada, using up what he'd thought was the last month of his visa allowance to visit the place where he'd heard timber wolves and bears might be seen. He hadn't cared about his own safety at that point; indeed, I had the impression he'd gone there to die.

He met with people, smoked—he was honest about that. Always a partaker of dope, he'd fallen in with a like-minded crowd and would have stayed there, giving up on the idea of suicide, instead finding a reason to live. His visa ran out, time ran out, but he stayed on. That was until he heard that some people were asking after him and in a panic left a place he'd called home.

With help from a couple of his friends, he was driven back south, somehow passing the Niagara Falls border and on to Cleveland, where he was dropped off one evening, far from home, a couple of hundred dollars in his wallet and an expired visa.

He had friends in Pittsburgh and knew he would be all right there. They would look after him for a while, keep him out of harm's way. The long drive, the looking over his shoulder and the constant worry had been too much. Exhausted, he bought his ticket at the bus station and just sat, keeping his eyes to the floor at all times, listening to the same tape over and over again, the headphones signalling he didn't want to talk to anyone. No, he didn't notice any other passengers—not until he had to turn off his Walkman to board the bus. He showed his ticket and was on his way to the far end of the aisle when a young woman smiled at him.

I leaned back in my chair, as did the lawyer. I caught his expression and smiled inwardly. This was a lot of information, a lot to check up on, but as I'd expected, Corrish had been forthcoming with every name on the journey so far.

"How long did you stay in the motel in Pittsburgh, the one you were seen going to?"

"No more than ten minutes."

"Why did you leave?"

"I don't like cockroaches."

He'd argued with the motel owner and got his money back. The owner even called the number Corrish asked him to, and within the hour, his friend turned up and drove him back to his place.

"Any witnesses?" I asked.

"His entire family, concerned for my welfare and a little put out by being woken up at such a time in the morning."

"What happened to Samantha after you left her on the bus?"

"I told her to hide underneath the seats while the driver did his spot check—she only had a ticket to Pittsburgh but was going on to New York. She must have been OK. As the bus pulled away, she sneaked a peek out of the window and blew me a kiss."

I stopped the interview there. I needed to know what happened after that, but this was already a lot of information to process at once. I had several witnesses to call, and if those all panned out as I believed they would, I would also have to make a phone call to a certain captain and tell him I was letting Ash Corrish go. There was so much sadness in the man—the complete opposite of my friend who had been so full of life, so cocky and arrogant. Corrish was not a man I could be friends with, but he also would not betray me in the way the good doctor had.

"How did she die?" he asked once more, and I found myself telling him that, as far as we knew, she wasn't dead, just missing. If I'd had even a shred of doubt in Corrish's innocence then his reaction would have seen it evaporate into dust and scatter to the winds. He slumped back in his chair and started to cry, and as he did, the fingers that had been constantly fidgeting, ceased and became still, rigid and tight. I turned off the recording and signalled to the constable, and we left him in the capable hands of his lawyer.

Outside, the constable was about to ask me a question when our chief stepped out of the observation room and quietly summed up his feelings, agreeing that Corrish had nothing to do with Samantha Ó Foghladh's disappearance—if his statement could be corroborated. I promised I would start my enquiries within the hour, I just needed to make a phone call first. When asked to whom, I could only reply: to Ash's sister.

Again, the constable drew breath to speak, and I was relieved when the chief issued him a series of commands, enjoying the sense of downfall in his demeanour as he was instructed to get Corrish some food and drink—"He may still be under arrest, but he is entitled to a level of decency from us after his ordeal." I could feel the resentment burning in the soul of the constable, the barely repressed urge to shout that he was nobody's errand boy.

Over the following hour, I made several phone calls, beginning with the university. I spoke to the dean personally, calming him down, promising him there was not going to be another scandal.

"Good," the dean said. "The faculty cannot afford another one after *your* friend's death."

I liked the way he emphasised the word 'your'. Yes, he had been *my* friend, but as I pointed out to the dean, he'd also made the university a lot of money—a kind of protection racket—and had continued to do so after his death, given the sales of his books had reached a level they had not seen in the last couple of years of his life. The dean put the phone down on me, slamming it so hard I imagined it shook the oak desk he was so proud of apart.

I left a message for Corrish's sister, asking her to call me on my personal number at her earliest convenience. Next, I rang my friend in Holland. I wanted her to tell me about the man claiming to be her cousin. Something was not right about all of this, and I wondered why she had involved me. The line rang out several times, and I was again forced to leave a message for my Magpie, Aakster. I ended it with my usual thanks and hopes and looked back over my phone records, realising she hadn't contacted me in over a week. She had never gone that long without some sort of message or call, and I felt ashamed for not noticing. She was young enough to be my daughter, and I loved her as any father should.

I was concerned enough to call her mother and ask if all was well. Her phone also rang out continuously, the only difference being it didn't defer to an answering machine. I made one more call, this time to a police station near Aakster's home in Haarlem and asked if they could send someone over to knock on the door, tell them I had been trying to contact them.

Chapter Six

I Asked Baudelaire, What Is Art?

Catherine Ó Foghladh

I IMPLORED HER SO many times to leave him behind, to walk away from the madness he had brought to the house—the drunken brawls, the odd way he would console us as children with a gentle hand upon the knee as he pushed his psychosis onto us, the slap around the face when he didn't get his own way, the punch to the stomach I received when I found I was pregnant, and the punch to the back of Samantha's head when he caught her kissing a black boy from school. He was evil, and that was only the half of it.

I walked away with a promise of an education in Europe, one that I made the most of. I didn't need his permission; I would not have asked for it. I just decided to go, but it meant that I left Samantha behind, and it was a move I deeply regretted every day.

Paris, such a city. I was taken with it the moment I stepped onto the train station platform. Such vibrancy, a different way of expression than I had ever seen or experienced in Cleveland. I was able to start again there, and I did…for a while. I'd gotten into debt, the lifestyle too exotic a drug for me. I'd met people I had no right to even gaze upon. I was introduced to those who'd obviously thought I was someone else, and perhaps they had a point, as I became that someone in the end. Looking out of the window to my office where campaign posters show my public face to the world, endorsements flood in, I chair meetings and am and held in reverence, I acknowledge this is what Paris taught me. Confidence.

It was a confidence I had to earn, and I had wanted to share the secret with Samantha. Not the bad days. Not the moments when, to avoid starving, I would beg or scour the for scraps of change beneath the beauty of the Eiffel Tower. I learned how to sell photographs of couples and get the money in advance for what was a two-penny adornment but one that lasted in some cases, as the relationship I had captured I posted to their home address…not before I had sent that address to a third party and received a percentage, albeit a fraction, of what they had been able to take from the property while the couple were declaring their love overlooking the city that was made for it.

I had become part of a network. I wasn't proud, but I also didn't want to go home, not yet—not ever if I had the choice.

At first, all went well. I studied French art—something both my sister and I were fond of—but studying comes at a price, and I soon realised that my attempts to capture the soul of Paris through my brushwork was underwhelming, disastrous even. I could pick my way through the finer points of the subject, and my dedication to the coursework was enough to keep me in my position, but I would never become a painter myself, despite people always telling me I had a flair for it.

The second Christmas I was in Paris was the hardest. Somehow, I had lost my grant and was forced to borrow at a rate I could not afford. While Paris was the most beautiful place I could imagine, it also had a dark, sinister streak which pushed the desperate to where they always avoided treading.

I found myself hanging around the edges of Montmartre, recoiling at the thought of having stooped so low I was contemplating joining this underground trade— one I had managed to avoid despite my father's demands. My first encounter earned me a black eye. I didn't even get as far as negotiating a price. We went into the shadows of an alley behind a restaurant frequented by rich English tourists convinced their pronunciation was passable and not in the least offensive, and where the price of a bottle of wine would have seen me eat for days.

I leaned forward to kiss the stranger, only to be pressed back against the wall and have a fist connect with my face. A hand over my mouth covered my initial scream while his other hand rummaged around my person. I had seen the looks of some of the girls my father knew when they told me of the shakedown they'd received, the rough free fumble, the man's belief that he could take what the girl owned, gratis. Those girls feared for their lives.

I was fortunate. My assailant was under the illusion that I was a professional girl, not some novice to whom some bread would have been like gold. As he pulled his hand away and hit me again, rendering me almost unconscious, I heard him whisper in the dark to someone I hadn't seen, "*Ça ne peut pas être bon, cette putain est pauvre.*"

I was poor, I had no money; that alone saved my life.

Almost an hour went by before I found the strength of will to get back on my feet and face the degrading stares of those dining outside the restaurant. I stumbled past, not catching anyone's eye but hearing the mutter and the under-the-breath condemnation of my plight, the bruises on my face already showing and a veil of blood drifting slowly down to my chin, the odd droplet finding its way to my T-shirt, adding a kaleidoscope effect to the print.

Unsteadily, I walked towards Rue Gabrielle and felt the eyes of the world upon me. I had fallen so far. Gone were the images that had romanticised what I believed would happen in such instances—the viewpoint of the woman caught in the overpowering gaze of male dominance as she lay upon a bed more suited to a queen than a prostitute, a study in female seduction by Henri Gervex. Or perhaps standing, dressed in black and with an approachable face as I surveyed my empire of alcoholics and the tears of regretful realism that sometimes adorned the champagne magnums sparkling with wit and damnation at the Folies-Bergère, a man asking me the price but caught out by a suggestive wink and the triumphant laughter of those who saw past the joke.

I was nothing more than a caricature, a travesty of the period, *Drowned! Drowned!* as Solomon would have had me portrayed.

I refused to go this way. I would not go home—I could not go home. I should just depart. Nothing to live for, I would die with dignity and place myself in the pose of Ophelia, an Englishman's ideal, to whom we owe the platitude of frozen beauty. Yet it only reminded me of the folly of love, of being at the mercy of man's perverted sense of revenge, my father speaking to me from across the ocean, the fist to the stomach and the baby I lost—a revenge for falling pregnant to a rival.

I struggled down the hill, hiding my face from those who tried to peek under the hood I wore, my jacket appearing as if someone had poured a particularly bad vintage of vinegary, sweet red over me in recognition of my poor waitress skills. I imagined the Sorbonne, the music, a city that survived a war and had been the envy of the world, the most electrifying place in which I could have lived: it would be an honour to die here.

I approached the Seine with tears in my eyes. I had no steel in my actions, no money for a drink to calm my nerves. If I was to do this then it should be quick; hold my breath under the water and let myself drift off in the dark.

In films, the heroine either dies or she lives, and a heroine was how I saw myself. If a heroine should survive at that point, she is rescued by one who dives into the river after her. Her clothes, torn a little, reveal a heart that ultimately wants to live, and her saviour comes to love her, and she, him…

Life is not that cruel or romantic. Instead, it offers a second chance in the simplest of exchanges.

As I stood looking down at the lifeblood of Paris, as fear gave way to certainty and I prepared to say goodbye, an open voice, strong but shrouded in a thick accent, bade me *salam*. There was no sound in my head that greeted this simple acknowledgement of my existence, no fanfare of music as the heroine turned on her heels and saw the man who had saved her and whom she would later marry. This was not a man who would have permitted such notions, but he was a man of his word, and as I studied him briefly, I knew I had been saved.

You can shake the hands of all the heroes you want. You can pose a smile and point at them as the photographer grins at their luck in finding the one person for whom that night the stars shine brightly, but to understand someone like Marshall Rhagodidae, to hear him speak with fire in his belly and with elegance in his belief—that is the true mark of admiration for destiny having called upon you when all you wanted to do was die.

He had just been sitting there, on the wall, a cigarette between the thumb and forefinger of his left hand, a small plume of smoke leaving his mouth as if the first rumblings of a volcano had been sighted by the populace below, igniting the nervous anticipation of what would follow.

He said nothing, just took another drag of his cigarette and smiled. Then he held out his hand, and I took it. I felt safe. For the first time in months, I felt as if I had a friend and that everything would be all right. He exuded confidence, and as he gently tended to my face, he took off his jacket and put it around me to keep out the cold.

It was the first act of kindness but not the last, and while I didn't see him every day, sometimes not for weeks, he always phoned me. He took care of my debt; he reintroduced me to important people. The only concession he asked of me was loyalty, and it was one I gave gladly. Some men do all that for a woman and believe they own her, that sex is the currency of exchange, but what is art? What is any relationship across the whole of human history? Just goods and services exchanged, and if you don't have the money then you pay in other ways.

For the man who saved my life by just saying hello, I paid in a different way, but so did he. I was under no illusion that I was the only woman in his life. That didn't bother me; it still doesn't. I had my tuition paid, and I ate well. In return, I was the glory on his arm at functions. I became a mistress without the expectation of sex, and I revelled in the responsibility of the moment.

After I graduated, I went on several trips with him. Slowly, I learned more about the man and I still wanted to be by his side. His was a vast business empire built not on the advent of the internet, Silicon Valley expertise and economic powerhouses trading blows over currency and gold, but on a habit, the illusion of the desperate in the decline of their faded dreams and their wish to numb the pain of modern society. I had wanted to drown and stare at the night sky through wide-open eyes; these people wanted to live but with their eyes closed and their senses dulled, their heads buried in the snow-white sand, nose down, sniffing each grain.

As soon as my sister turned eighteen, I sent her the money to get to New York and from there to get a plane to Paris. So little to remember: just walk out, get on a bus, be circumspect, don't pay any attention to anyone, focus on the future. It would have all been so easy. Get to Paris, ring Dad, tell him your safe with me and you're never coming back. I would have added *until you drop dead*, but Samantha was not that mean. She was a dreamer, and despite all he had done to her, she still wanted to love him.

Then the phone call came from New York. Holed up in a cheap motel room, she told me she had no money for the plane ticket. All I had sent her had been lost, her purse stolen as she hitchhiked from Philadelphia and took a lift from a man who ditched her at a drive-through while she used the restroom. All she had left on her was a hundred bucks: she'd managed to get to New York and pay for a room for one night, but that was it. She was going to call Dad. It took several collect calls, but I convinced her to get to the airport and wait there for me. I would take the first plane out and fix the problem.

As I stare out now from my office window and see the shape of the city I want to bring to fruition, I can openly admit it was the first of many problems. She had confessed she had struck out at our father—an ornament to hand smashed into his skull. He had become violent, possessive. Driven by a deep-seated resentment, he had taken to going through her possessions and had unearthed her money and her passport. He wasn't dead—she didn't think so anyway—but he certainly wasn't in good shape. She had left him there at the table, out cold but breathing.

I could not take care of this on my own. For the first time since the night when the waters of the Seine distorted my reflection showing not the doomed rose of Ophelia but one of the grotesques that guarded many a Paris church, I reached out to my benefactor and asked him for a favour. He didn't hesitate. Of course he would help solve the problem—did I need money for the extra plane tickets? I didn't. I had done well under his wing and had a steady, indeed lucrative income. I required help with a problem of greater significance. I needed to send my dad a message: he was not to look for Samantha again or I would report him to the authorities and see him locked up. Could he do that? Of course. Marshall had people he could call upon at will to deliver a message in every town.

An alarm goes off on the desk behind me, reminding me I have a date with the Board of Trade and Drinks and my number one fan, the police captain. What is the price of art? Just prostitution! We are all prostituting ourselves for some greater glory, and those who are happy to sit in the mire of the moment are the worst whores of all. They turn tricks to stay alive. I have played the game and come out on top. I *will* find out who delivered the message to my father, and I will see that pathetic Englishman suffer for it. My dear Samantha, you would have enjoyed it all. There was a lot of fun to be had, a new beginning for you, risen again from the depths of the Cleveland streets. Why did you have to change the plan?

It has been a good day. I have a murderer in my sights, and after all my hard work, after losing my one true friend who never wanted anything from me but loyalty, I will finally be the top bitch in my hometown. I am going to make a lot of people regret that they allowed my dad to get away with so much. There's no denying I hated the bastard, but to go into the polls for the biggest job of my life…well, I need to settle an account or two and put the past firmly where it belongs: underground and allowed to decay instead of rotting in the open air where someone, anyone might come across it and resurrect the ghosts of my past. For if that happened, I would not be seen as the Pierre-Paul Prud'hon Justice and Divine Vengeance Pursuing Crime; I would be holding hands with frauds in the Eighth Circle of Hell.

Chapter Seven

The Way That the Dead Tell Tales

A Father's Story of How He Died

I CAME TO DURING the early hours of the morning, the lack of fire in the grate having turned the house cold, listless, argumentative. My head hurt, and as I put my hand to where the pain was coming from and felt the reminder of the night before where my daughter had hit me with one of the few ornaments her mother had brought into the house, I found my anger still raging.

Samantha, I curse you, child, and if you walk back into this house today, I will skin you alive.

I needed a drink, some painkillers.

I eased myself up from the position she had left me in, slumped face-down, blood congealing during the hours I had been unconscious, left to rot. Ungrateful bitch. And after all I had done for her.

I found some leftover bourbon in the cupboard next to the fridge, the painkillers a little harder to come by until I remembered she kept some in a drawer beside the television. Groping in the mess of a teenage girl's life in search of putting an end to the ache is not a way to deal with the early morning cold, but then neither is finding a wad of money in an envelope and a passport bearing your daughter's name.

Where is she? Has she really just left me here?

A sudden thought occurred to me: I'd had her money in my hand when she struck me, her passport on the table in front of me, staring at me, mocking me. Staggering back through to the living room, I saw nothing.

I came to again a few hours later, the headache still buzzing in my ears like a hornet caught in a tumble dryer, just at the point of finding an escape route and then making every human on the planet pay by stinging them over and over again until they dropped dead. I picked myself up off the floor and was thankful I hadn't broken anything. Why had I fallen? I remembered nothing after…the money, the passport. I looked around under the chair where I'd been sitting when I confronted Samantha.

Being disoriented in the face of overwhelming facts is the final proof that you have been suckered into being the tail on the donkey. I had been sideswiped by my own daughter, dealt a bum set of cards and told to lay every cent I owned on the table…

The money. Where was the money? There was a couple of grand at least in that bundle. Had she taken it from my safe? That was payment, fees for the syndicate.

I felt the back of my head again and discovered it was no longer bleeding. It gave me more reason to feel resentment. She had left me alive…*the money. Think about revenge later, check the safe first. Panic…the key.* The key wasn't around my neck on the chain Samantha's mom bought for me. *Bitch. She's taken that too.* Unsteadily, I staggered across the room and to the bottom of the stairs. I pulled back the loose-fitting latch on the fourth and fifth step and saw with relief that the safe was closed, locked. So where was the key?

Thirsty but concerned for the welfare of the money, I half zigzagged towards the kitchen, bumping into the table, taking down a chair as my grip refused to let go. There, on the floor, my chain and the key. It must have come off, or perhaps the bitch tried to get it from me, but something had stopped her.

I needed water. I filled a glass with water from the tap, then again, and a third time, breathing heavily, then puked my guts up in the sink, the water pink, not deep, but enough to know I had been in a fight. I tried to open my eyes against the strain of the sun; the pain was terrifying.

Another glass of water, wash out your gut. It's not serious. Do I need medical attention? Possibly, but who has the money for that? Roll on, big Bill Clinton, that wuss Bush let the side down.

My thoughts would not string together properly. I thought I saw movement in the yard, but it was sweat, nothing but good old-fashioned sweat catching my left eye's attention. I puked again and determined that the blood-to-water ratio had reduced. I sat down, collapsed really, on the cold, chipped floor, twisted to one side and picked up the key before puking a final time but with the force of a bullet, and for a while, everything went grey.

Time means nothing to me. It is the dollar earned in the time it takes to put a bullet in a man's gut, a moment in which to slit his throat. A few thousand of those, hell, you can set up a prostitution ring so tight it would make your hair stand on end.

I keep my eyes closed. The day's moved on. Birdsong in the distance—brave little fuckers. I'm surprised there are any that bother 'round here. Everything is dirt, nothing grows, just weeds, human weeds that need cutting down, treating with poison, and I offer that poison as a package deal.

I hadn't noticed the back door was open.

Slowly, I pulled myself up, using the cupboard door as a lever, and looked into the metal sink, a festering pool of stained mud disguised as blood. My guts ached and it took several long breaths away from the sink before I felt the focus coming back.

Plan, can I manage a plan? Of course! I own this area. I can do anything, just not control a screaming girl, it seems. Where did that thought come from? Was that doubt or just the well of anger that refused to settle down?

Thinking still in short bursts, OK, the brain took a hell of a beating, no surprise there, but Ó Foghladh, you old dog, you can out-think anyone, even in this condition. Close the door, fill the kettle, find the bleach, go to the safe, check the contents… Where did she get a passport from? Her sister, of course.

Samantha has no money of her own—unless she stole it. I thought I taught her better than that. But I'll be generous. I won't kill her. I'll make her my new partner.

Sweet Samantha, your daddy loves you. Come home, darling girl. I will turn over a new leaf, cut the booze, the gambling, the extortion, the drugs, the prostitutes. I will do all that for you, ha-ha. If it wasn't for this headache, I'd laugh out loud. She'd better come home today or she will be dead.

I shut the door and locked it. I had gotten halfway to the stairs when I remembered I hadn't filled the kettle, damn head.

Fuck it. The gap in the stairs was still open. Bending down, I put the key into the lock of the safe and wedged it open. All the money was there; my Aladdin's cave of deceit was fully stocked.

So the money must have come from her sister. That's two punches to the guts ready to order. Who should I call? The police will have a field day if they come over, though some of them owe me money…an equal trade. Find my daughter and we call it quits?

A noise.

Another one: closer, from the kitchen.

I walked through, this time sure of my footing, and stopped as the door banged itself against the wall. I had locked that; I clearly remembered doing it. Then again, the last day had been one of excitement, hadn't it? So much fun—smacked around the head by a girl, finding out she was leaving me… *After all I've done for you. I kept the men away from you, didn't I? Or most of them. I didn't let the junkies sleep with you, the ones covered in sores. No girl of mine's getting a disease… But I let one get pregnant. What was the man's name now?*

A noise came from behind me, and I turned too quickly, nothing but stars before my eyes, dancing pinpricks in the static, and then a knock at the door.

I hadn't realised I had been out so long until I reached the front door and saw paper scattered across the yard—more than just a daily. The news was everywhere, pages scuffed as if people had wiped their feet on them to get the monotony of life out of their shoes. I looked at the date on each one. *Three days. Three fucking days! She'll be long gone by now. I've lost my sweet.*

Another knock on the door, and even with a mind that was running on half fumes and spit, I took the precaution of looking through the spyhole. *An Indian. What the hell does he want?*

I pulled a face. I remember doing that. I didn't trust their scrawny asses and their high and mighty attitudes. Deep down, they were as liable to screw you over as a newly bankrupted man telling his favourite mistress he just needs to borrow the diamonds for insurance purposes. I had known plenty of them, not recently though, not since I'd last been to a casino and lost all my money to the smiling chiefs. I'd hit out, but those boys were fast, and while I know I knocked a tooth out of one, in return I was treated to a fractured jaw and came to in a town thirty miles away from the action.

A clearing of a throat behind me and another of those brothers stood proud and erect, dressed in jeans and baseball shirt, straight-faced, not a hair moving. He motioned me to open the door as he held out the welcoming committee of a small shotgun. His smile was the most unnerving sight I had ever seen, even beating the time at high school when one of the farm girls had walked the school halls with the severed head of a bloated adult male pig in her hand, a sharp butcher's knife dripping with blood stuck between its teeth.

I still remember her yelling frantically, "He committed suicide! He committed suicide, it's OK!" And then, as she reached our classroom door, she stood perfectly still, took the knife out of the pig's gluttonous mouth and slit her own throat. It turned out her dad had done himself in the previous night. He'd set fire to the pig barn to claim on the insurance, not realising the gasoline had splashed over his shoes and the bottom of his pants, and as the fire raged, so did he, burned alive and smelling of roast pork. The girl was so traumatised she dismembered one of the few pigs that had survived and then brought it to school, even while the firemen battled to put out the fire.

That didn't give me nightmares, but an Indian pointing a gun at me? I almost took a dump in my pants there and then.

I backed up towards the door, suddenly alive, the head clearing quickly, but I was trapped. I just hoped that it was a warning.

I knew where it had come from. I knew Marshall's hand anywhere, that damned spider. I opened the door and stepped back towards the other brother behind me as the other walked in, calmly shut the door, looked around the mess on the floor and signs of struggle and asked, without any irony in his voice, if I'd had a party.

I heard the one behind me say he had found the safe. I raised an eyebrow, knowing he had been in a long while before I'd closed the door, but he hadn't found the safe. I had left it open as my brain stuttered to get working again. I asked, knowing the answer immediately, "Rhagodidae?" It was always going to be him, the dark figure whose voice I heard always with an English accent even though he was from the East somewhere. I swear he did it on purpose, knowing I hated the English as much as I detested the Indians.

"He sends his regards," I was told. "But he needs to know something. Why have you been withholding tax?" The words spat like acid off the tongue of the one who came through the front door. From behind, I felt the tip of a knife go into the small of my back. I held firm, trying to figure a way out of this, even as they severed my thumbs with a small, blunt saw on the table where it seemed like only yesterday I had woken up with a blinding headache and a dip in my skull.

I held my nerve as they tied my hands behind my back and stared dead-eyed into my soul. It was when they started pushing the first knife into my eyes that I cried out, begging for the first time in my life to *please stop*. I had never even done that when my mother, having caught me taking money from her purse for the first time, whipped me with a leather strap that bit into my legs, cutting deep and leaving welts that took a month to heal.

The second blade went into my other eye. They had held it open long enough for my pupil to dilate, to take in the sharpness of the metal as it gleamed in the duty of their service. Then slowly, with care, they pushed it into my eye, causing me this time not to bargain but to swear, to cuss them out, to call these two motherfuckers every name I had in my head. I think they took offence at that, as one of them withdrew the knife from my eye, and as the black fog of unconsciousness closed in, I felt them start to slice into my tongue—revenge exacted for my racist outburst. I clenched my jaw as they tried to pry my lips apart. I was not given them this pleasure, and despite being on the verge of death, I fought like a bull...until they jammed my mouth open and cut my tongue across and then down towards the tip, leaving it lopsided, hanging out as if I was chowing down on a corndog.

I could not sob, I could not cry. My stomach heaved as the blood gushed down my throat, creating hell right here in Cleveland. I faintly heard them rummaging through the house, the money already pocketed, their laughter and chatter grating at what senses I had left. There was nothing else to take—a diary of names, perhaps, useful contacts should they ever tire of being pawns in another king's game of chess. *Good luck to them. I hope they get syphilis*, I thought, a final act of petulant aggression keeping me company in a world turning cold.

Then, as if it had not happened, there was silence, a quiet moment of solitude in which I felt my heart getting weaker, grasping at the weight of eternity that awaited me. Only then did I feel the brush of a lip against my ear.

"Rhagodidae thanks you for the partnership. You have been a comrade in this fight, but you see, times have become tough. Please accept this act against you as severance pay, pale-face." Then a hearty, almost hippo-like laugh from the other. Apparently, I was the butt of a joke, the final punch line, as he repeated the other's line and I worked out he'd called me that because all the blood had finally left my head, congregating in two different rival camps, some on the floor, most in my stomach and lungs. I was drowning.

They left quietly. I heard the door being pulled shut with a gentle touch, and then like timber wolves, they stole away into the night. They wouldn't be caught.

The last thought that entered my head was that I was sorry. *Sorry I ever hurt you, ever laid a finger on you, took you to a darker place. My baby girl, Daddy was wrong. Daddy was wrong…*and as the blood finally slowed to a trickle and I felt my heartbeat give way to silence, I thought of the girl who bought a severed pig's head to school one day and whose father would have smelled of pork when they buried his remains, and I begged forgiveness from my dear, sweet Catherine.

Chapter Eight

The Secrets We Keep Hidden

A Sister's Tale

IT WAS THAT night all over again. I dreaded receiving a call when he went away to find his roots, so far from home. Anything could have happened, but back then, I had my mother to calm my nerves. When I felt anxious, I would turn to her for guidance, to reassure me, to keep me afloat. And when that did happen, when we got the call that he had been arrested for outstaying his visa, my mother dealt with it all. She made phone calls; she got in touch with some old friends, who called their friends, who by some miracle managed to get him off with just a warning and a ban from travelling to the United States for a period of time. Not that it mattered; he never wanted to go back, or so he told us.

Now, nearly thirty years on, we hear he is in trouble again. I say *we*: this time, I will have to deal with it. Thankfully, Mum no longer knows what day it is, let alone who I am. I doubt she would even remember Ashkii—well, maybe not her son, but she certainly remembers her dad.

It is typical of Ashkii to get in trouble like this, always so selfish, never a care for what it might do to those he left behind, the worry, the scandal…now this.

Oh, the detective who rang me seemed very sincere in his apology, a hint of regret in his voice as he informed me of what had transpired that morning, although it was reassuring to hear him say that as far as he was concerned the evidence was flimsy, and Ashkii had been very forthcoming. He'd even given the detective a list of names to call, addresses. Typical, really. The only places we knew he had been were New York and New Jersey at the start and ignominious end of his journey. Did I know the people he stayed with in Pittsburgh? Why he went to Cleveland?

"Anywhere, any clue, Ms. Corrish—it is vital that we have something to corroborate his story. While I believe him, there is a captain of police out there who seems to want to hang him out to dry."

The detective's words chilled me. I tried to think, flustered as if my admission of guilt was being heard down the complex of wires, my confession that when it came down to it, I didn't know that part of my brother's life.

Could I help with a period of time for which there is no record, between university and what he did next? This time, I stalled, my heart in my mouth. Yes, of course I could, but what did that have to do with anything? He came home a few months after the girl disappeared, yes, but he was diligent in his studies, only the strain of it all coming out towards the end of his second year, and by then he had taken his final exam. The pressure had become so intense we had to find a space for him for a while.

That year, once again, Mum dealt with the fallout as if she was unstoppable, always on hand, visiting him as often as the facility would allow. She has always had his back, using the wandering-spirit excuse more times than I cared to remember. I'd thought it was going to be all right. He secured a good job, was urged to take on a promotion…to move away. That last one came from me.

I convinced myself that I had noticed Mum becoming ill, that it would be better if he wasn't there to get under my feet, told him I would look after her in the way she had looked after me when the fear threatened to overwhelm me. *You go, all will be well…* Truth be told, I just wanted him gone, to not have that habit of his of tapping his fingers against anything solid, from left to right, as his mental capacity was tested.

She is so near the end now.

Part of me would like to scurry away, to just tell the detective I am so very sorry but I cannot help, my mum is dying and I know nothing about my brother's whereabouts. *Screw him*, my inner voice screams, and I have to breathe twice and listen carefully to the detective's next question to make sure I hadn't said it out loud.

Did he ever talk of this girl to me? Not to me, he didn't. I don't know if he did to Mum. If he had, she never uttered a single word to me about it, never disclosed his secrets. I made my excuses—errands to run while the local nurse is here going over Mum's charts. He seemed to understand, a certain sadness in his voice as he reiterated if there was anything I remembered then I could call him anytime; it was likely Ashkii would be released on bail by the end of the day, tomorrow at the latest, but it would help if I thought of anything at all.

I made pleasant noises, assurances, and when I was quite sure the phone call was disconnected, I swore at the top of my voice. It was so abrupt and unlike me that the nurse poked her head around the door and enquired if everything was all right. I explained, in semi-truths, that my brother had got into a spot of bother abroad and had been questioned regarding some incident at the university.

She frowned at that but then reminded me why he was out there: to replace a senior lecturer who had died at the hands of a drug cartel. "Not in any serious trouble, I hope?"

Well, we can all hope that. I smiled and reassured her. "Just some small thing regarding qualifications. Stupid boy neglected to take proof of his work—all will be well."

I told the nurse that if she was all right for half an hour then I would go and get some fresh air. Another stuffy night indoors I could do without. I laughed it off, not the first time where my brother was concerned. Before she had time to argue or ask any further questions, I slipped on my coat, picked up my purse from the dining room table and waved goodbye, telling her I wouldn't be long, adding, "Help yourself to tea." Help yourself to tea—the British answer for everything. In the space of one short phone call, I had been reduced to a simpering caricature of life hindered by my island mentality.

I walked around the village, smiled at the vicar as she sat in her front garden talking to herself, practising her address for the following Sunday and asked her how her wife was doing, where was she now. Oh, well, indeed the refugee crisis certainly needed all the volunteer helpers they could get. Several washed ashore last week? A boat full of the poor unfortunates found just a few miles out to sea, clinging to life by the skin of their teeth— "Back in a couple of weeks' time, though, you will be pleased to hear."

I left her to her sermon, no doubt having earned a mention in her thoughts to God—something along the lines of wishing I would be a bit more careful about the insincerity I showed to the world when I didn't care what the answers were. I had known the woman for almost all my life. Before I found out she was a lesbian, I always thought she and my brother were a bit too close for comfort, always in each other's pockets. She was the reason he didn't go off to university at eighteen.

I went to the cake shop, passed several minutes with the young girl behind the counter, and then finally to the post office to get some writing paper and stamps. I tried to make it all seem normal. My brother was being questioned about a missing girl, my mother was dying, I cared not for the vicar nor her wife... Everything about today was far from normal, but I had to make a show of it. I smiled as I walked the short distance home, the flowers that hugged the country roadside catching the sunlight almost perfectly as the sun also made its way home.

It wasn't until I reached the garden gate that I noticed the vicar standing outside the door, the pain of concern etched on her face, her arms outstretched as if she were receiving me into her bedroom and a tear of misery trickling seductively down her left cheek.

I heard her say that she was sorry, that it had been a quick release, a final reminder of the brief call of life. I scowled at her. If she saw my response then she didn't let on. Then the nurse came to the door, hanging around like the Grim Reaper's younger sister, all tied-back hair and hand-wringing demeanour, stuttering that she had gone to take a small amount of blood after I had left the house and noticed that Mum had stopped breathing. No final revelations on her death bed, no final rage at the life she had lived, no denouncement of her son; just a final exhale of breath and quietly she slipped away to live out eternity trapped in the mind's soul.

The nurse had called for an ambulance straight away, but they would not be here for at least another half an hour; a motorway pile-up on the M40 had seen to that. She had looked out of the window to see if she could see me, figuring I would have gone down towards the bakery, then rang the vicar to see if she could stop me, but she had been too late, not being able to find the number before I made my briefest of small talks. The vicar had come straight over, which meant the errant son would find out before I wanted him to. I didn't want him to have this closure yet. I wanted it all for myself. I wanted to damn him for a while and feel able to blame him. I wanted to make him sit there in a cell and be ignorant of the fact that his mother had passed away.

I think the vicar knew that, or at least recognised the flush of anger on my face. It was one she had seen a few times since we were children, when I had pushed her off the swings in the village playground, when I had thrown an apple at her head one afternoon at the village fête, when I declared my feelings for her as a teenager and she turned me down, giggling with Ashkii about what I had told her. I pushed her over the following day at school, her knees skinned, full of gravel pits, the bruise and scab taking on the shape of a man's gallbladder that had seen too many stone deposits take root, a human pomegranate that joined the two halves of her legs together.

Every time, she found a reason to forgive me. Had I known then all that pardoning of my soul was because she entertained ideas of becoming a god-botherer, well, I would have championed Ashkii further to attempt to get into the stoic cow's knickers. It would have been entertaining to see him fall.

The vicar put her arm around me, and I was surprised to feel myself cry. I always thought that when Mum passed on, I would be brave. I had imagined the looks of admiration from the villagers and my mum's friends as they saw me patiently enduring my pain. But because of this woman's sincere humanity, I was denied this simple act of retribution to the village that had seen me become a spinster, second only in their thoughts to a man who ran away, who skulked off in pursuit of what? Family ties to a man who had died decades before we were born. I may have stayed home; I may have been a fixture in the village, first working at the small school, then in the library, rising to a good position and respected for the way I kept the building in top shape until the last council budget cuts, but he had always been the one they looked up to. He had escaped. He had seen a part of the world they could not begin to imagine as they pruned their hedges and washed their cars on a Sunday morning.

Even when he had his very public breakdown, he was still everybody's friend. He was the counsel, he was the ear, and he never judged. He was a fool, a weird, habit-controlled freak, but he was liked. If he had met the nurse, I am sure she would have loved him—I half suspected the vicar did as well; wife be damned, she would throw it all away for him, wouldn't she?

I shrugged off the consoling arm, not with a warning, not out of expressed unpleasantness, but because it reminded me of what

I had missed out on. I'd had my mum, but I'd never had a hand to hold except hers.

No help required. Yes, of course you can wait until the ambulance comes. Yes, Vicar, a prayer for Mum would be helpful. You are so kind to have always been so close by.

It was when she announced that she would ring Ashkii for me that…

That was the moment I stopped and looked at her in a mixture of bewilderment and frustration. I told her she didn't need to do that. I didn't want him disturbed until tomorrow, he had a lot on his plate at the moment, lots of work at the university. The nurse butted in, forgetting her place in all of this, saying that she thought I had said he was being questioned about a matter. The vicar raised an eyebrow, an action I once found alluring as a young woman. Her voice, always calm, sincere, cool, sympathetic, unless you told her that you loved her, spoke softly.

"Ash is in trouble?"

Her tone will forever haunt me. Part accusation, part understanding, she sensed my reluctance to involve him was born of anger, a zealous hatred and jealousy because he got to do what he wanted, and as far as I could see he'd messed it up every time. Smoking dope on a beach in New Jersey, hiding away in a New York kitchen, a trip to a sanatorium to ease his troubled mind. The only trouble he had was that of his own making—a thief of my time, of my mum's constant thoughts—even at the end she'd have been thinking of her precious Ashkii.

There it was again, that comforting arm around me. She led me into where my mother lay still, motionless, attracting the invisible horns that summoned her saviour. Tea soon arrived, made by the nurse as she kept an ear out for the ambulance. The vicar and I looked across my mum's dead body and stared into each other's eyes—the first time I had properly looked at her since we were teenage girls.

She told me not to worry, to give her the detective's number and she would call him this evening, that I must not blame myself. She knew deep down I loved Ash, just as she did. I stopped her there. I agreed to let her call and give what assistance she could, or at least ask them to pass on the message regarding his mother, but how could she say she loved him? As far as I was aware, they hadn't seen each other in years.

With the smile of a deceptive angel letting loose a sacred text to the unenlightened, she informed me they spoke two or three times a week, and that she had visited him when he was enduring his dark time. He'd even introduced her to her wife! A former colleague!

It was stuff I didn't know. Once again, I had been kept out of Ashkii's life. The real kick in the teeth came when she told me that my mum—*my own mother!*—had entrusted her with certain letters and correspondence that she had kept from Ashkii. The vicar had not told him; she'd been instructed to only pass them on once Mum was dead.

Trusting this woman instead of her own daughter… I was ready to violently break loose of any remaining shackles when two paramedics came in looking sheepish for the lateness but also shattered from the events that they had obviously had to clear up during the day.

The vicar excused herself, leaving the nurse to explain what had happened and to receive confirmation of how to proceed from that point. A sudden and final heart attack, not violent, just enough to shatter any remains of a life that had seen the birth of two children and the love of a husband, and which had withered away to nothing in her final, lonely hours.

Chapter Nine

One Letter in Particular

The Vicar

I AM SURROUNDED BY letters, postcards and the odd scribbled note declaring mischief. I am engulfed in the period of a man's life that stretches all the way back to when we were young children, mere phantasms of what we grew up to be, and it makes me want to cry.

I stayed with Annalise until it was time for her to go to the hospital, the nurse kindly taking her in her car, following at a respectful pace behind the ambulance, which took her mother, slowly but assuredly, to the hospital. I told Annalise I would think of her tonight in my prayers, and for the first time in quite a few years, as I made myself a pot of tea, I thought of her as much as I had done her brother all day.

What a family. Ash has always been my friend, and I could not have asked for one finer. He kept my secrets when we were younger; he showed me how to roll a joint; he kept me safe while we explored the woods together. We stayed out of sight from Annalise, hiding whenever we could or within an adult's eye line if we could not. I returned the favour: I implored him to go and explore the world. I wanted him to escape his sister's tyranny and destructive behaviour. I would be all right, I told him. I was getting away from the village as well—only as far as university, but it was enough miles between me and the tormenter.

When Ash came back, he was different, more self-conscious. Gone was the carefree nature that had drawn me to him as a child and young adult. On the outside, the village saw what it needed to see—a young hero returning home and ready to join the ranks of the over-educated, not yet ready to settle down, take over the local pub or even work a day collecting glasses, laughing and making fun of the regulars and being respectful to the visitors when it meant getting a good tip. No, this was a man-boy, in deed and in name.

The idol gossip machine went into overdrive when he had been sent home from America, driven no doubt by Annalise, but it had the opposite effect to that which I'm sure Annalise wanted, for if she had intended to make him appear a fool, then her plan completely missed the point. Ash had been popular before he left; all the people of our age group found him fascinating, and his name, which in other places would have been a hindrance instead became myth-like. The seven labours of Hercules, fourth task: get stoned on a beach in New Jersey and start a fight with the local police. Ashkii Corrish was a resounding leading man—even our parents couldn't help but love him.

I pick up a letter, sent from New York a few months after he left. My wife doesn't like me keeping these memories. It's our only source of disagreement, but to me, they symbolise the boy, on the face of it one who could have a local bar in stitches as he regaled them with jokes and performances, but behind the façade, he was unhappy, worn out, always in search of something he could be tied to away from Annalise. He begged me to keep his secrets, said he'd send any letters or correspondence to my university halls, and unless he said otherwise, I was not even to tell his mother where he was.

He was heading north, over the border. He had quit his job that night, taken some money from the safe—not a great deal but enough to keep him going for a while—and was heading to a place where he hoped he'd find spiritual awakening.

I knew what that meant when, one Friday afternoon between lectures, the porter thrust the letter into my hand as if it was the most important document I would receive in my life. Old-fashioned but lovely, the porter no doubt thought it was some declaration of love from a suitor; it was, but not in the way he was thinking.

For a while, the letters became sporadic. I once went a month without any word from him, and whilst this worried me, I imagined what it must be doing to Mrs. Corrish, who doted on him and could not see the harm in the boy. Annalise may have shown outward concern, but I knew it was only to mask her apathy and resentment.

Finally, I received a postcard: *On the move, will write when I get to Pittsburgh. Love you, Ash.* Just enough to stop me from admitting my sins to his mother, enough to make me smile. As promised, a letter came about a week later. He was with friends that we had met at a Genesis concert a couple of years before. Surprised to receive a phone call from him in the middle of the night, they had come straight away to pick him up and look after him. He was full of talk about this girl he had met on the bus who was travelling from Cleveland to Paris, a beautiful girl who touched his heart with her honesty in a way that he had only ever felt with me, the difference being, I guess, that she might in time sleep with him, whereas I would need to have been drunk and he a girl to even consider the possibility. Still, it hurt that he had found someone, even fleetingly, and I wasn't there to see it happen, only hearing about it as if it were second-hand news, the rumour of his actions.

His letters drifted in frequency from there on, a few as he walked from Pittsburgh to Philadelphia, none for two months, then almost every day while he was in New Jersey. One of the final communications from him during that period was to ask if I had ever heard from the girl, the one on the bus.

Nobody writes letters anymore, and yet he still does. Only occasionally do I get a phone call. A letter, though, that is permanent, a gesture of commitment from which I could build a fort, right here on the study floor. If they should fall, I would be buried alive, not found until someone needed to talk about a wedding, the Christmas fête or my wife returned home from one of her trips to save the world.

I received letters twice a week when he was placed in care, and I matched those with my own visits to see him. I eagerly awaited the postman's knock when he got married, having fought him, desperate for him to avoid making the mistake of marrying a woman with the same destructive personality as his sister. Mercifully, she did him no real lasting harm, not compared to his sister's manipulations and mind games, and I was relieved when, after a year, he turned up on my doorstep and asked if he could stay the night. Through the crack in the bathroom door and the steam that rose and tried in vain to engulf him, I saw the battle scars of his time with her, and when I told my wife about it, she began to look upon Ash more kindly, using the same soft tone she had at the beginning, before things became complicated.

Letters come, bills require payment, and there is always some drama in the village to sort, but Ash's documents of his life were always welcome, especially when he found the job in Malta, teaching English literature—a new pace, a chance to change his life. I didn't have the heart to reply to his letters in any way that would rouse his suspicion that his mother was dying. I knew damned well that Annalise had no intention of relaying the news, and for as much as I didn't like her, it was not my place to tell tales, no matter how wicked she was.

It was my duty to be there today, though, to comfort the soul of one who had lost a part of themselves, but it doesn't mean I wanted to be near her. I loved their mother; she was an aunt to me, generous, quick-witted, funny. By contrast, Annalise is sullen, moody, desperate and quick to turn, and the day she made a pass at me when we were teenagers, I wanted to be sick.

She had seen me kiss a girl from school, one of those more easily outspoken girls from the larger council estate in the nearest town. Stupidly, I thought no one was watching, but you can always bank on Annalise to witness all, and it triggered something in her. She was not attracted to me; she just wanted to have something over me, a way to control me as she did Ash. She was spiteful, threatening to tell my mother if I didn't. I ran off into the woods with her voice screaming after me, imploring me to come back, that she didn't mean it, come back and talk…

It was Ash who found me, by accident, I'm sure, but then he always has a knack of knowing when his sister has been at the centre of a storm. She tells anyone who will listen that I laughed in her face. She tidies it up as a schoolgirl crush, a mere fancy, but I didn't laugh and that was no declaration of love. It was sinister, spider-like, a set of fangs ready to tear into flesh. Logic was always suited to Ash: own it, he said, I know you're gay. He suggested I tell my mum that night, cut the poison out straight away, my mum would understand, and if the village turned their back on me, he never would.

Part of me thinks he did that to finally have something on his sister, to see Annalise squirm in the mud bath of her own making, slipping easily back into the pit each time she thought she was getting out of it. I watched his eyes blaze in the gathering gloom of the evening. He wanted this more than anything else at that point, and I eventually shared his need.

All these letters…the one I am looking for must be amongst them. There is time, though. He won't be going anywhere tonight. I thought he would be safe. The accusation was awful, but if he was in the company of a good man then it was better than him sitting at home. His habit of coping when under stress would have surfaced, and if he was going to do something silly… well, better to not be alone.

As soon as I arrived home, I rang the detective and explained the situation. He took down my number and told me he would call back in a few minutes; he was just going to confirm my details with Ash and his lawyer. As good as his word, he told me that Ash had given him permission to tell me all that had happened—that he had been accused not only of abduction but of murder. I heard the detective say these words, but they were unrecognisable. This wasn't Ash.

"Unless there is proof, some sort of corroboration…" His words hung in the air like underwear on a washing line, for all the neighbours to see.

"I have letters." Those three words came gambolling out of my mouth. It's true. I have one letter in particular that will show he was not with the girl when she disappeared, and if she is dead, it is not at the hands of Ash Corrish. In amongst these handwritten keepsakes is the evidence—a note from Paris proving she made it out of the country.

People go missing every day. It is human nature to either belong or to be by ourselves. Several years of training, a devotion to the way of God—I think of such things in terms of lost sheep. Ash is lost. He has always been so. Neither one thing nor the other. He makes jokes, but he finds them full of torture. He says he was born wrong, a cruel hybrid, and it was only through embracing his heritage that he found his way to being part of a community again.

He has always been in turmoil. His sister, the sainted, in her own eyes, Annalise abused him when he was small, yet he had managed to move beyond that. His mother must have stepped in at some point, but it's always there in the background, always there gnawing away at him, and while I know he is innocent of this crime, there are others that both Ash and I covered up, making us both culpable, both guilty.

Find me the letter… Is that my voice or the detective's? It could even be Ash's—pleading, insistent, damaged, all connected, do unto others as they have done unto you. During the time he was in care, he struck out, disconnected for a while. His letters were rambling, confused, full of regret and damnation. On one visit, I was allowed to enter the facility but then turned away with a polite but firm shake of the hand. He had tried to take his own life, something I believe he's always fought against. I found out later it was a reaction to seeing one of the other patients in there, a woman so deranged by drug use that she would find ways to whisper into the ears of the less fortunate about all the dreams she had of her dead son, needles stuck into every inch of his tiny body.

In amongst the last of the piles of mail and communications I have surrounded myself with, I finally find the one I'm looking for. I opened it when it arrived, giving way to temptation and the desire of the unexplained. The small gap where I plunged a knife into its soul and watched as the contents spilled out is ready to mock me again, to convince the world I am nothing more than a snoop, a friend who cannot be trusted. I didn't think I was ever going to have to explain to my friend that I had heard from this Samantha, that the letter he had been waiting for had arrived, no return address, no forwarding number, just a signed declaration that she didn't want him to look for her. She was happy in Paris; she had met someone; thanks for the company on the bus and sharing your music for a while, but now please, leave me alone.

One page of paper posted in Paris a couple of weeks after she was last seen on the bus in Pittsburgh. It may as well have been a death warrant to Ash, soaked in blood and delivered by the cruellest of hearts. I could see her point. She didn't know Ash, but he had been taken with her in a way I have never seen him with anyone else, even eclipsing the woman he met in Philadelphia who took him under her wing for a while and one day came to England for a visit and stayed, with me. Who became my wife.

I nervously pick up the phone and dial the detective's number. I owe Ash this, for all the times I could not help him before.

I owe him thanks and help. No answer, I try again and each time it cuts to voicemail. On the fourth attempt, I leave a message, though I would rather talk to a human being.

Tired from the evening's excitement, I stretch out and make a mental note to clear the past away in the morning, perhaps even take the time to sort the letters in date order.

I fall asleep knowing that my friend is safe. I have proof of his innocence in my hand, tightly gripped so I will not lose it, and my phone ready to answer on the table by my side.

I would like to say on record, with God as my witness, that I didn't hear the phone during the night. It is only the next morning, when I am woken by urgent, frantic banging on the vicarage door that I realise I have missed several calls from the detective. I open my bedroom window to see what the commotion is.

Below me, rage and hate blazing across the village, Annalise Corrish's angry words hit me square in the stomach. Her brother has been attacked and is in the hospital. He isn't expected to live.

My poor Ash, what have I done?

I tell Annalise I'll be down as quick as I can and shut the window as my phone rings. I answer the call immediately. It is the detective.

Chapter Ten

A Handful of Nothing

The Ohio Captain

I MISSED THE BEAT at times, but sitting in that chair had its advantages. What it didn't have was control over everything that came across my desk—I could no longer hold anyone accountable for the crimes they'd committed. The other problem I had was that my natural urge to see the system work meant I'd had to become part of it in order to break it apart, to smash it into tiny fragments and set them on fire. There is no place for corruption in any police force.

I learned late last night that the detective in charge of handling the case in Malta was considering releasing Corrish—not enough evidence to hold him. Indeed, there were rumours of verification that he could not have killed or even abducted Samantha Ó Foghladh. I asked one simple thing, but because I couldn't control it from here, I was left with my feet dangling in waters churning with circling piranhas. I listened to the information coming across the wires and had to stop myself several times from slamming the desk with my fist.

Calmly. I thanked my informant for the news, and then—after a suitable few minutes of throwing bottles of water at the office walls, grinding down the anger as each one shattered, raining shards of glass on the room, some embedding themselves into the wood of my desk—I phoned Catherine Ó Foghladh to tell her the news.

If she was pissed, she didn't let it show. Would this affect the investigation into her father's murder? I was surprised that was her first concern. I'd been expecting a good five minutes of swearing and pleading while I made all the right noises to placate her distress and came up with a way to salvage the operation.

The Maltese detective had asked all the right questions relating to Samantha's disappearance and listened to Corrish with open judgement. He'd left for an hour or so, gone back and made what I can only describe as lip-service enquiries into Ó Foghladh Senior's murder. No look of terror on Corrish's face. Confused, yes, but no reaction to him having been finally connected with the serious, brutal death of a Cleveland citizen. The detective believed him, and Corrish had shown no outward or obvious signs of stress.

I don't know how they do it in Europe, but this was not happening. I had filed the correct paperwork; I had sent across the relevant information. He was the guy. I knew it, those assholes in Malta must have known it—had I missed something in my efforts to see Catherine get the job she wanted? Had I been blind to the truth?

She was saying my name again. Not my given name—not even the shortened version of it, which she sometimes allowed to slip out over dinner or drinks—but my professional designation, with added emphasis on *Captain*. She wanted to know if I'd followed through on everything that the police in New Jersey had sent. Of course I had, but there were inconsistencies, too many witnesses who had since died. The woman who had sold the ticket to Samantha had died a few years back and hadn't recognised the boy. According to her, Samantha had been sitting alone, quietly surveying the scene. I remember her telling me that she'd watched her because she didn't want her to come to any further harm. She'd described Samantha as frail and looking as though she had been in a fight already, but the boy, this Ashkii Corrish, wasn't with her.

Catherine insisted I tell her exactly what had been said, what message had been relayed from the man in Malta—"I want my father's murderer found. I want to go into the election with a clean slate, to be able to look the people in the eye and give them some sort of closure. Understand?" I almost replied with just her forename but thought better of it, kept it professional.

She hung up, and I was left wondering. Mindful of the mess I had made with the glass, I searched the building for a broom, anything to get the remains of the moment out of sight before the office cleaners found another way to report me to human resources. Had I been blindsided, and for what reason would Catherine Ó Foghladh want to cause such an incident? I fought against the instinct to protect her. Yes, she badly wanted to win the election. She stood on a promise of restoring the public's faith in law and order—a contract with the people I fully endorsed. I had stood by her side for months. I had smiled and held her hand aloft in recognition. I wasn't allowed to get political, but as my time was coming to an end and my bosses thought it was good to show mutual interest in this day and age, they saw no problem with me working out my final days alongside Ms. Ó Foghladh.

I found the broom and pan—my detective skills were on high alert, it seemed, or perhaps that was all I was good for now, taking out the trash. I am not a young man, and I wanted this to happen for Catherine. More importantly, I wanted it to work for me—to leave at the end of the election with my reputation intact and take up a private post as Catherine's head of security: fewer hours, less pressure, more money to work with, no overtime bans, no letting good people down, no office politics, no smashed glass—I had forgotten the towels for the water.

The woman who'd sold Samantha the bus ticket may have been dead, but the driver who took her at least as far as Pittsburgh, if not further, was still alive, as were a couple of others on the arrest list in New Jersey.

I tidied my office, all evidence of wrongdoing, of my mistake erased, except there was still the chain of evidence. Wet green towels—how would I explain those if someone were to ask? There was the broken glass…well, I tripped over, and the bottles smashed to the floor. Why did you trip over? What caused your moment of carelessness? Why is your office wall damp if the bottles fell off the desk? Why is that one piece of glass embedded in your desk? Not like you to go dizzy—think you should go for a medical? What if…what if… My head was pounding, and my collar felt tight against my neck. I had to sit down, take a tablet, spray relief under my tongue.

The truth of it was…I needed to retire. The years had taken their toll on my health. My marriage was down the pan, and yet she wouldn't leave. Good Catholic woman that she was, she spent more time kneeling on the hard floor of the local church, scrubbing away before the altar, looking up at her saviour with smiles and dedication, than she did at home. She was just waiting for the day I was found dead in my office, when that grumbling pain that had dogged me for a while took me off to the other place—not where she plans to spend her ever-after. I'll be playing cards with the devil as evening turns to night while she's getting roses delivered from God every morning.

The nitroglycerine spray had done its job. I sat in my chair and closed my eyes for a while, allowing my concerns to get in the way of facts. I may well have been heading for a lifetime of playing poker with a weak hand in hell's casino, but at least I wouldn't be bored.

Was it too late to ring the driver of the bus? He was an old man now, probably in bed, sound asleep and dreaming of days when he was a knight of the road, driving between cities, picking up waifs and strays who couldn't afford a car or who wanted the anonymity. You could pretend to be anyone on those buses.

The bus. How did the boy get to Cleveland? He hadn't come from New York, where he'd landed some months before, but until he ended up in New Jersey, nobody knew where he had been. Only the inconvenience of being caught up in an investigation had pinpointed his whereabouts.

He hadn't been in Cleveland long, I was certain of that. A day, perhaps two at the most. But what if he had just arrived? What if he'd dropped off there? I turned on my computer and looked at the bus routes that led to the city. If he had been dropped off, why not Buffalo? Why not back in New York, where had he come from beforehand? He surely would not have come north just to go south again. That made no sense. To the west…well, you really have to want to travel out that way in the first place. From Canada? And if he had not arrived in Cleveland by bus…

I was not in the flush of youth. My heart was not used to this kind of abuse anymore. I wanted out of the game, but I was also entranced by the question. I added the name of a detective I knew in Canada to that of the driver.

What had possessed me to say I was related to this Dutch woman? It had been Catherine's idea—would it come back to bite me on the ass? I didn't know. I tried to look her up on social media to find nothing but empty static. I was loath to access any police file, but I did find a picture of her in *The Times of Malta* online, standing next to the detective as they gave evidence in the case of the death of one Marshall Rhagodidae.

I knew that name. It was there, nibbling at the back of my mind, creeping about by stealth, holding a knife to my memory, but I could not shine a spotlight on it. I had heard it somewhere, or read it…dammit. *Let it boil of its own accord, it will come.* According to the online piece, Marshall Rhagodidae was notorious in Europe, head of a drugs cartel that had seen him rise to power at a time when heroin was sweeping the continent. Of Afghan and British descent, he'd committed suicide in the tunnels beneath Valetta and was strongly suspected of murdering the detective's wife as well as being behind the death of one of the detective's friends.

No other chatter, though, which was odd, almost as if it had been suppressed, much like the name in my mind.

I thought about calling my wife but, like the bus driver, she was more than likely fast asleep. Praying to God was taxing on the soul—when had we drifted to the point of seemingly no return? Would she be concerned if I called at such an hour? Would she console me, find a way to smooth things over? There were days when I wanted to believe she still cared, that her crabby tone was just a ploy; she was forever imploring me to take note, to come back to her. I could do that—if I retired as soon as this was over and didn't take up the position with Catherine.

I had phone calls to make, too early yet to call the detective in Malta, and anyway, I would have to explain myself. I needed to call these other numbers first, starting with my helpful friends in New Jersey. I looked down at the number that had called me and then at my email, which contained the information they had sent over. There was a discrepancy—had I been tired or had I just become so inept, my judgement clouded by the desire to close a case nobody else had cared about?

The email had all the hallmarks of being authentic, just enough information on Ashkii Corrish to make someone with a vested interest feel as if they had finally made a breakthrough; enough to make them feel important. However, the area code was different than last time. It was probably nothing, just circumstance, but 609 and 201 are vastly different. One was right: Ocean City was where it should have come from; but 201—that was a whole different ballpark.

I called the number in the email first, answered as I expected by local police. The woman who answered, a nightshift worker who suffered from insomnia and whose husband was a beat cop, was helpful. She looked up the old case for me and remarked it was the second time the information had been requested. I asked her if she was sure. "Of course, honey. I don't forget when I'm asked to look up information on someone I knew."

She knew Corrish? How was that? I realised my hand was gripping the phone as tight as a man holding his chest when the inevitable strikes; I had been played.

"Corrish was a lonely guy—wouldn't hook up with any of us local girls but loved hanging out with us. We took him in—we were so sorry when he was deported."

I asked what reason the other officer had given for wanting the information. Her answer stung me.

"Honey, he was no cop. He was a journalist writing a piece on academics who teach in foreign countries—you know? Part of that whole Brexit thing."

She had gotten permission to dig into the man's past—what did it matter? They saw no harm, and all her friends were excited to hear Corrish had done so well—"If you speak to him, tell him Anna and the gang say hi."

I ended the call, but not before thanking her and asking if she could write down all that she remembered about Corrish, and about the conversation with the journalist, and send it to me directly. She replied she would and signed off with a cheerful goodbye. I wasn't cheerful. My chest grew tight; I had a lot to think about.

Why had I taken it all at face value? What sort of example had I set to my protégés keeping faith with the way I dealt with corruption?

Dammit, I need to call the detective, damn the hour. I would have to come clean and tell him I had been duped…turned over by Catherine. Why had she insisted I tell him I was the cousin of someone he once worked with? Was it just to get his cooperation and get this case moving? She said she wanted closure, needed it to drive home the message that law and order were the top of her priority list.

Too many thoughts swirling in my head, I reached for the remaining bottle of water and felt it slip through my fingers.

I saw it in slow motion topple off my desk and fall to the floor. The crash resounded in my ears as my mind closed down.

I was found slumped in my chair, alive but unconscious. My wife was called, and an ambulance came quickly. A quiet night in the city of Cleveland—I figured it was a trade. I lived to make amends, and someone innocent had to die. By the time I was at the hospital and on a gurney, I was awake enough to insist on making a call. I phoned the detective in Malta and told him what I had found. I spoke quickly, not mentioning at this point my deception which had brought him into the case. He was silent throughout. Did he know? Was he about to take a stab at the remaining working parts of my heart?

When, finally, he spoke, he told me there had been an incident. Corrish had been attacked the previous evening, not long after he'd been released. Evidence had turned up that Samantha had made it to Paris. Corrish was not my man.

Chapter Eleven

Robbed on the Way to New York

Part of a Missing Woman's Journal

How can a plan descend into madness in such a short time? New York is a crazy place, full of desperation, a smell I cannot get out of my nostrils and buzzing with an energy that makes me think that if I truly wanted to escape, then perhaps I would be better off here rather than skulking in my sister's shadow. I owe even getting here to a New Yorker. Well, I thought so at first. Turns out I know how to spot a Brit in need of conversation.

The journey had started well. I ducked down underneath the chair and stayed out of sight as the passengers, including the boy, departed into the Pittsburgh night. My smallish frame made it easier to hide in such a manner, and the only person I believed had seen me do so was one of the Amish women; the slight smile on her lips as I resurfaced sometime later told me she would not give me away.

If I had been caught riding the bus for nothing, I would have been arrested, sent back home. I could have given a different address, but my name was on file, my fingerprints on record, thanks to my dad. With no ticket beyond Pittsburgh, I was going to have to find a way to leave without having been seen. Mile after mile rolled beneath our feet. A minute passed by into five and on towards an hour. I had no plan. I had hoped that I was just going to be able to get off in Philadelphia and make a run for it, but as soon as my unwitting companion left, I felt the confidence drain from my soul.

I closed my eyes and prayed. In the same way I asked God to give me strength when I hit my father with the ornament, I prayed for a sign now. I don't know if I believe in such things, but it gave me comfort and it allowed the Amish woman who had been smiling at me when I was hidden under the seats to take a chance and sit beside me.

I returned her smile, and when she asked if I was already missing my friend, I could not help but be drawn into conversation. Unlike the boy, I told this woman the truth, the whole top drawer. I don't know if it was because she was of a faith I could not get my head around but didn't want to upset her, or because underneath those garments and cultural constraints, she was a woman who understood.

She took it all in, occasionally glancing around to see if the man who accompanied them was listening. Only two of her company were awake, and they did not shift in their position, blocking the view of anyone curious enough to find our conversation interesting. She was horrified at what I had done to my father. I could not blame her—if I had been in her shoes, I would have probably done a lot more than gasp. But she understood. She took my hand and lowered her head awhile, praying for me. I let my head drop in the same manner, but I didn't pray, not at that point. Her words were enough for the both of us.

When she finished, she asked what my plans were. It was the only lie I told her. I said I was going to New York. "A girl can get lost there, can die there," was her calm rebuke. She wrote down a number for me. "If you get there, call this number. He is a good man and has looked after several of our family during their rumspringa. I raised my right eyebrow and smiled; she blushed a deep, fiery red, and answered my unspoken question: "Yes, he looked after me too before I realised that what I wanted from life was to be with my family."

We discussed how I was going to get off the bus without being seen. I still had plenty of money so would be all right to get to New York. I had some in my purse and some squirrelled away in my pockets—the just-in-case money. She looked around to make sure all was in order behind her and then leaned in close to my ear and whispered, "When we get to the rest stop at the Sideling Hill Road, wait for my signal, but you will have to be quick."

I held her hand, and for a brief moment, she held it in the way it was intended, before breaking off and returning to her seat, making sure I understood the simplicity of her plan. I put the phone number she had given me into my pocket and gripped tight my bag.

An announcement just a few miles out from Sideling Hill brought the remaining passengers on the bus to their senses, and I looked for my friend. She had disappeared. A small moment of panic threatened to envelop me. The toilet door at the back of the bus opened slightly, revealing a shaft of light and a beckoning finger. I got up and walked towards it, still clutching my bag. Sneaking a look back down the bus, I hurriedly slid into the tight, cramped space that passed for peace and tranquillity on a heavy route and saw my new friend standing there in only the undergarments that her faith provided. She held out her clothes and urged me to put them on and take her place in her seat. I dressed at speed, pulling her clothes over the top of mine, all the while thinking this was the most insane thing I had done in my life.

I got a look of mild concern from my friend, and she told me to leave my bag with her until I was off the bus and then to double back, shove the clothes through the narrow slit of the window, and she would get my bag to me. Her sister would depart to talk to the driver while she left my bag underneath the bus, ready to be collected.

This was not only insane, it was reckless. I was trusting my life to someone I barely knew. But then I saw her smile, her eyes dancing in the greyness of what she had once more become, and I understood her need for the adventure, even a sliver, of what she had once tasted.

It was to be quick, smooth; the headcount had to be right. If I had got off the bus without any sense of having belonged there, the authorities would have some idea of what I had done at Pittsburgh and where to start looking. I had to act brave, like I fit in; I left the toilet with my head held in a pose of meekness and servitude, right past the driver who was talking to an attendant at the service station. He smiled, making a comment about needing some air, and then clapped the attendant on the back before he went off to find a restroom for himself. The attendant kept an eye on the bus, making sure those who boarded were in possession of a valid ticket, but ignored me completely as I walked around the side and to the back window, which was slightly ajar. Through the gloom, I could see a pair of warm eyes searching for me.

I removed the plain fabric dress and the white bonnet and stuffed them quickly through the gap in the window, heard a brief utterance of thank you, and then the window closed. I hung around at the back of the bus: this part of the escape had worked out fine, but I still needed my bag. I needn't have worried. When the driver returned, a steaming cup of coffee grasped in his hand, two of the other Amish women made a scene of asking questions, directing attention away from my new friend coming up behind them and first dropping the bag to the floor and then kicking it underneath the bus. I bent down to see where it had ended up and saw it had cleared the tyres. If I followed the bus out, I could pick it up and then disappear into the night.

My father had luck on his side for most of his life. He'd avoided arrest on countless occasions. In the end, he was so well connected that the police stopped bothering. Some even became part of his payroll, funded by someone I never met, but with enough power to cause problems in high office. We never had much; he was not that kind of man to care enough. What he liked was fucking the system over. I know he had some money knocking around, but I never saw where it was hidden. He had been smacked around when he was younger and had learned to fight back, never again letting a blow land on him…until I decided enough was enough and found the strength to beat him.

It was with that same luck, rotten to the core and one day sure to catch up with me, that I picked up my bag without anyone giving me a second glance. I wondered about the kindness of the Amish woman. I hadn't gotten to know her properly. I didn't know her history, why she had returned to the community after her year away, but she helped me. I had met two good people. I felt blessed and confident I was going to do this unscathed.

I hitchhiked for an hour before finally getting a lift from a scruffy man in a broken-down wreck of a car, but beggars cannot be choosers in this life. Seeing as it had started to rain, I went against my instinct to walk away and took the seat that was offered. The car smelled bad, the man worse. He had that glint of trouble in his eye, and I kept my hand on the door latch at all times. He spoke quietly, grimly, as if talking hurt his teeth. He offered me a cigarette; I refused warily. He objected but didn't make a fuss, instead reached across and unlatched the glove compartment to reveal a small bottle of vodka. I'd had nothing to drink for hours and the sense of thirst was overpowering, intense. I took it from him and took only a sip, enough to cure my mouth of dust.

He urged me to take another drink, but I just smiled, handed him back the bottle and told him I was all right. He seemed satisfied and we continued all the way to Philadelphia with no further awkwardness, though I still kept my hand on the door's latch in case I needed to jump out quickly. I made polite conversation when necessary, but this was the polar opposite of the ease with which the boy and I had communicated. I needed to keep my wits sharp: I had spotted the barrel of a gun in his glove box; if he pulled it on me at any point then I had to be ready.

We drove into Philadelphia during the early hours. He parked and I thanked him. I offered him some money, but he refused, saying it was good to help a sister out. I smiled again, perhaps out of relief that I had made it this far. A train to New York was my next leg. As I stepped out of the car, my bag across my shoulder, and bent down to say thanks once more, a motorbike came out of nowhere and blocked my escape. I had been so consumed with relief to have made it out of the car unscathed that I'd forgotten to look for any other danger. In a new city, there is always the possibility of being mugged, especially in these days of desperation,

The driver of the car tried to get out to help me, but he was too late. Another bike pulled up beside him, and a gun was shoved through the window. He was told to sit tight. I don't blame him for doing as he was told at that point. *Take the bag*, I thought. *It only contains some clothes.* As long as he didn't take my purse, which was under my coat, I would be fine. The flash of the blade was quick and tore right through the strap in a second. The knife came up towards my eye, the early rays of the sun making it glint, then it was gone. The two bikes took off, and I was left with a shell-shocked man and my purse for company.

I got back in and sat breathing heavily for a moment. "Can you get me to the station, please?" were the only words I could find.

He was as good as gold. Any bad vibes I may have gotten from him initially had now rolled away. He was in shock but was still all right to drive. Perhaps long after I had left him, he found a way to let go of the rage—I would not be surprised to hear he'd exacted some revenge or at least taken himself to the gun range and fired off several rounds straight at the target. Guns have always concerned me, but as we drove along towards the train station, I knew he was going to do something reckless.

I looked in my purse: my small journal, the tape from the boy, my money, some other effects—everything was there except my passport. I don't know why I didn't keep it on me. I thought about it on the train to New York, and I still couldn't find a reason. Perhaps deep down it was because I don't think I intended to use it.

The man in the car dropped me off at the station. This time, I looked to make sure no one was going to jump me, and I ran straight in, pulling the hood over my hair and eyes before I paid for a ticket with cash and then bought some food and drink. I was starved and needed something quick. I fished out the phone number given to me on board the bus, and with my hands beginning to shake from my ordeal, I dialled the number and asked the person on the other end of the line if he could help me.

It took several minutes to explain who I was, not wanting to give too much information lest this new cog was to prove a dodgy connection, but all was good so far. He spoke briefly, told me where to meet him when I reached New York, who to look out for.

I didn't give him the right time of when I was going to arrive; I wanted to get there early, check he was alone and make sure this wasn't a trap. It was, after all, part of the finale of my adventure. I was now passportless—no identification, no proof of who I was—and for the first time that didn't make me feel nervous. Oh, I was worried about what I'd tell my sister when I called her. She'd figure something out, though. She always knew what to say and do. Gone was the frightened girl who, at sixteen, got pregnant to an off-duty cop and lost the baby when our dad punched her in the stomach. In her letters, she was more confident, alert, and that actually frightened me more.

New York. You could lose yourself here and never be seen again.

Chapter Twelve

The Longest Night

The Detective

I COULD BARELY KEEP my eyes open. What a night, the likes of which I haven't experienced since before my friend died. Not since his yacht blew up and sank in the harbour of the three cities had I felt such absolute exhaustion, but I could not sleep it off. I had to stay awake, at least until Corrish came out of surgery. It had already been a stressful day and evening; now this. Poor Corrish was battered inside the transfer room by what appeared to be a random attack. I had only stepped out to make some calls and send a few messages regarding the situation; I could not have predicted any of this would happen.

We had interviewed Corrish again, not under caution this time: it was plain to me that he was innocent. I wanted to learn a little more about the man, but after half an hour, we'd both had enough. He'd told me all he knew, and I was prepared to let him leave; my chief agreed and told me to place him in the transfer room.

In the time between, I phoned the captain in Cleveland and made him aware of our situation. To say he was unhappy would be understating it. He was furious, almost apoplectic—I didn't doubt for a second that had I been in front of him, he would have throttled me. As it was, I was able to tell him that if he had problems with the way I'd dealt with procedure then he should talk to my chief. I ended the call with a curt goodbye.

Next, I tried to contact the woman acting on behalf of Corrish's sister only to hear the continued dull silence of my unanswered request for conversation, in the middle of which I received a text from Aakster's mother, apologising for not being in when I'd tried to call earlier on in the day and assuring me all was well.

I admit I had pressing concerns that far outweighed the possibility of drama in another country, and had my eyes been on the ball, I would have sensed there was something not right in that message. We had come to know each other well enough that she would call me regardless of the time of day, and the message was bland, lacking the usual familiarity of our interchange. I let it go when my attention turned to the shouts of a couple of constables in need of help. I sprinted back towards the station and saw Corrish on the floor, being kicked by a man who outweighed him by an easy fifty kilogrammes, most of those muscle. I didn't recognise the man, but he was doing severe damage, his foot connecting twice with Corrish's head before I reached them.

I received no answer to my immediate question of what had happened. One constable staggered backwards in agony, falling against the wall, his nose broken and blood gushing down his young face. I urged the other officer to use force: a truncheon to the back of the assailant's knee; failing that, and without reprimand, another part of his anatomy. I tried my best to heave the attacker away, but he was too strong, a monster of a man, and it took six of us to restrain him, including my chief who, in his youth, had played rugby semi-professionally in Italy.

I hurried to Corrish. He wasn't dead, but he may as well have been. He had taken a hell of a beating. His face was badly bruised, I was sure he had several broken ribs, and his breathing was erratic. The desk sergeant phoned for an ambulance, and as the unknown assailant struggled against a combined force of police, I remember thinking that Corrish would be dead before he got anywhere near the main hospital—even making it to one of the closer smaller ones was doubtful. I knelt beside him and tried to keep him comfortable, but I was fighting a losing battle. No matter what he had been accused of, he was still in my care.

The man who had committed the vicious assault was still struggling when the paramedics arrived; with a nod from the chief, one of them took a syringe from his bag and jabbed it into the man's hefty left bicep. I watched him weaken, his struggle becoming less fierce. He finally stopped as they were putting Corrish into the ambulance; his vitals were precarious, I was told, but they would do what they could.

I stared in disbelief at my chief and received the same look of incredulity straight back, neither of us understanding what had happened. The unexpected escalation had left one man close to death. The chief ordered me to go with Corrish, and I didn't wait to be told twice; he would deal with the situation at the station and call me as soon as he had anything concrete to go on. As I climbed into the back of the ambulance and watched the paramedics fight valiantly to save Corrish's life, I wondered how my colleagues would hold that man down for questioning when he finally came around. Poor Corrish hadn't stood a chance, like a twig against the force of a hurricane.

The journey seemed to go on forever, broken only by the shout of one of the paramedics informing all on board that we were losing him. I received a text from the chief telling me they had cuffed Corrish's attacker, but nobody could lift him; all they had managed to do was sit him up against a wall and tie his feet together. Completely unorthodox, but the chief had no other options.

We arrived at the hospital and the surgeon allowed me to remain with Corrish in case he regained consciousness and could tell me anything useful. I suspected my presence was futile, that Corrish would not regain any awareness at all.

My initial thoughts were proved correct. The blows to the head should have killed him; his ribs were broken in several places, and he also had a ruptured spleen. Only the intervention of a damn fine surgeon stopped him from bleeding to death. If he lived, he would be in pain for quite some time.

The surgeon suggested I go home, get some rest. Corrish was not going anywhere. I thanked him but refused. Whilst I had been watching the surgical team save Corrish's life, I had wondered about the nature of the attack. Nothing like it had ever happened before, not in my time anyway. Yes, we'd had a gunman kill a witness on the steps, and we'd seen civic unrest, but we had never had someone walk into the building and lay the human equivalent of a truck on somebody else.

I phoned the chief and let it ring for a while. When, finally, he answered, he sounded as tired as I was. In the background, I could hear the prisoner ranting about his rights. I raised my voice and asked the chief if he had looked at the security footage yet. Somebody had to have let the man through, he could not have got in there by his own accord. The answer was as I'd expected: all information wiped, we had a problem inside the station.

I'd vowed when I returned to duty that this sort of corruption would be a thing of the past. Now someone, or even a group of people, had made my word seem nothing, empty. I didn't like the sensation that was crawling in my stomach. I barely heard the chief ask if Corrish had woken up yet; a nurse put her finger to her lips as she passed me, alerting me to my loud shout of "No!" More quietly, I relayed the news that Corrish was out of surgery but it was still touch and go, bid my farewells and told the chief I would call again later.

Others would be awake now. I telephoned the vicar in England several times to no avail, unsure of how to break the news to Corrish's sister. Nevertheless, I called her next and was surprised when it was answered on the first ring. She had been up all night, unable to sleep despite having been prescribed sleeping tablets. This latest news was a blow, but not in the way I'd expected. She seemed to take it personally, as if her brother had done it to overshadow the grief of losing their mother.

I pulled my ear away from the phone. Her verbal diatribe against Corrish was astonishing, calling him for every name she could think of, some novel to me. When she finally calmed down enough for me to apologise for bringing her the bad news, I went on to say I had tried to call the vicar but was getting no answer, would she mind going to check on her and ask her to call me?

That prompted yet another outburst, and I prepared for her to descend into a stuttering oral cascade of colour, but she soon regained her composure and told me it would be her pleasure to see what the sainted vicar was up to.

I suddenly felt bad for the woman on the receiving end of that meeting, who had probably spent an exhausting night looking for the proof she was sure she possessed and now had a tornado heading her way. I wondered if I should warn the local police; I could imagine a second beating being delivered that morning, this time supplied by the edge of a caustic, even poisonous tongue. The poor vicar wouldn't stand a chance.

My next call would have been to the captain in Cleveland, but he called me first. He sounded weak, apologetic. In much the same way that events had unfolded with disarming abruptness here, so too had his life changed since we last spoke. Through small breaks, which I was soon to learn was him breathing into an oxygen mask, he informed me he'd had a mild cardiac arrest, not enough to strike him down in fear of his God, but one that told me he had assessed the situation and made a few changes to his earlier conviction. I liked that in the man: anyone who can see beyond their own backside eventually has to have a shred of decency in them.

I told him Corrish had been attacked but was out of surgery now and under guard. I didn't tell him that the guard was just me. I didn't tell him anything that might tip the balance towards full-blown regret. I had my suspicions, though they were not directed at Captain Holt. He asked for the number of the vicar in England; he wanted to talk to her. I almost wished him good luck getting her to answer the call but thought I had already done enough damage on that score today, so I told him I would clear it with the chief and send him the number if permitted.

Only then did I sit back in the chair. I revisited all I knew, which admittedly was not much. The trouble with only ever seeing the story from your perspective is that unless someone tells you theirs then you may as well be firing blanks into the air, and there was something I was missing, some small piece of information which might point the finger in a certain direction.

The chief texted me an hour later—I must have fallen asleep—with news about the man who attacked Corrish, a Sicilian by all accounts. I thought it apt that he held the name which struck fear into those with long memories: Capone, the Rooster. And then came the kick in the teeth. He had been at one time affiliated with an old friend of mine. Marshall Rhagodidae—the Spider. Even now, eighteen months after his death, he had the effrontery to plague me.

The attack had all the hallmarks of Rhagodidae, which meant this was a hit paid for by someone with the same connections. How did this Rooster get into our coop, though? That certainly meant there was someone on the inside. I thought we had scrubbed the place clean of such infections, yet the virus had stayed hidden in the shadows. Somebody wanted Corrish to take the fall for something he hadn't done so they could profit from it. I could only see one person fitting that bill.

I mulled over this for some time, only dragged out of my thoughts when my phone vibrated. It was the vicar from England, and she was in obvious distress. She told me she had received a call from America just as Ash's sister arrived at her house accusing her of dereliction of duty. The captain, she said, had begged her for forgiveness and told her he would be interested to learn, if possible, of the proof she had of Corrish's innocence so he could show it to the dead girl's sister, finishing with a promise he would make amends. Was he all right, she had asked, and his answer made her anxious and sad. She broke down in tears as she recounted to me that he'd replied he really didn't know and asked her if she would pray for him.

Annalise Corrish, on the other hand, had been truly awful. She had raised enough of a war outside the vicar's house that neighbours who never saw that time of the morning were jostling, craning their necks to see what the latest village set-to was about. Those with long memories of the antagonism between the two women relished the idea of 'some kind of spiritual cat fight', most hoping the vicar would finally 'put down Ms. Corrish and denounce her as Satan'.

I hadn't meant to laugh at that image and apologised. With kindness and a little laughter herself, the vicar told me not to worry. She went on to explain she had spent all night looking for the letter and had fallen asleep, which was unforgivable, but the memories had been overwhelming, crushing. She had, however, found the letter proving that the young woman had made it to Paris and that Ash could not have abducted or killed her.

She must have sensed my excitement because before I could ask her if she would go to her nearest police station and get them to verify it and send it over to me, she told me she was on the way to the airport. One of the very few direct flights to the island from the UK was that afternoon, and she would be in Malta by evening. Could I meet her at the airport and then take her to the hospital so she could sit with her friend?

I didn't have the heart to turn her down. I assured her gently that it would be fine, that I would get the chief to sit with Ash while I came to collect her. I wrote down her flight details and warned her to be careful. Whilst my trust in my American counterpart had improved, there were still people out there who could hurt her if they knew who she was and what she was doing.

"After what Annalise did to me this morning, they cannot scare me," was her upbeat reply.

I wished her good fortune and prayed that the evidence she had was as conclusive as she thought.

Chapter Thirteen

Let Me Introduce Myself

Marshall Rhagodidae

CONTRARY TO POPULAR belief, the counterculture never went away, it just became franchised. There have to be some benefits to doing someone a favour; by being kind to them once in a while, you get to enjoy their loyalty. You can play on that—serve them the finest cuisine one night and for the next week serve them offcuts from the rankest offal, and they won't complain. It is the same in any business: greet them with a smile and firm handshake, and they will look to you for inspiration; deliver every so often and they will laud you from the heavens while you sink them further into the mire. Bit by bit, moment by erotic moment, you turn them on, tune them in and then watch as they drop out, destroyed by their own greed.

You, my dear Catherine…oh, how different you are. You never really asked for anything, didn't fall under my spell. You only allowed me to catch you for a brief second, enough to make the pleasure worth it, your skin shining in the reflection of the Paris water, the insane belief that your life was over, you poor runaway, starving, broke—could I save your life tonight?

That independence I admired, and you have kept it going like a nursery rhyme sung by infants, never growing tired, never wavering in the ability to sing out loud and make others hear you. You became the toast of Paris, my second-in-command, although, of course, I never let you know it.

That is why it was my pleasure to help you in your true hour of need. I arranged the flight, I arranged another passport for you. I even had my driver pick you up and take you to the airport. I was so sorry I could not be there be with you, to comfort you, to hold your hand and whisper into your American ear that it was all going to work out right. I couldn't be there because while you were picking up the forged documents I was already heading out to New York to take care of the problem myself.

I didn't want your sister here. I didn't want your attention diverted by someone who didn't even have the fortitude to seek a way out without your help, aside from which, I wanted your father to suffer yet again. He had lost you; let him lose the other one, this time for good.

I love air travel. So much more refined than getting in a car and dragging on fumes from oversize exhausts. Trains... well, everybody loves a time of romance and nostalgia, but the airplanes, now they are a luxury I cannot skimp on. Anything that takes away from the memory of sitting upon a camel's hump, anything that stops you from worrying about the possibility of spider bites—the solifugae, whilst not venomous, delivers a nasty reminder of nature's power over the weakness of men. That has to be a good thing, right?

I was a young man, barely in my twenties, when I saw what a bite can do, not from a solifugae—which merely hangs to the hairs of camels when you ride them as daylight catches their legs and scuttling eyes—but an army, an invasion force bent on taking my country apart. It is not the first time: the British, after all, tried so desperately to control us, to do to Afghanistan as they did to India. Then, of course, the Soviets piled in, cocksure of their place in the world, and as with the British, and with the Americans to come, we refused to give up easily.

I will not see my work unravelled. I will not witness history in such fashion as when Nur Mohammed Taraki was assassinated, nor on the day when I turned twenty-one and saw the Brezhnev

Doctrine take effect. I hate the British, the Americans, Western powers, the arrogance of Russian intervention. But what I hate most is having my life interrupted because one girl cannot find a way to leave hers behind without help from a big sister.

There is always time for tea; there is always time to make a toast: here's to you, Samantha Ó Foghladh. May you enjoy life.

Growing up in Afghanistan would seem like the end of the world to so many of these children, these spoilt rich kids. May they all die at the hands of the heroin I produce. Let them all become slaves: here's to them.

I kissed Catherine's hand as we parted. I left her in a small Parisian café, not far from where I had first spied her trying her level best to be something less than what she really was. I did not interfere when I saw her lead that man down the alleyway. I thought she might die, and at that point, it was no loss, another dumb foreign girl playing at being a woman. I sneered as I drank my coffee and immediately dismissed her from my mind, preferring to watch a group of people on an adjoining table enjoy themselves, get drunk, take in the best of Paris. Aside from two of the party who spoke with ease to the waitress and even apologised for their friends' behaviour, they made fools of themselves as they devoured horse believing it to be prime steak. I liked the two who tried to speak the language of their hosts. It wasn't perfect, but it showed willingness, honesty. Shame they were English.

Still, I was impressed enough to make what I thought was just going to be a moment's small talk with the couple. I asked why they had not told their friends that they were eating horse. The man shrugged and replied in his best French that they would not have believed him; they were looked down upon by those in their party. I smiled and played sympathetic overtones, deflecting my humour so it went unnoticed by the rest of the table. I bought them a bottle of champagne: the best in the house for my two new friends, soiled vinegar substitute for the rest. My friend was right; they wouldn't have noticed anyway.

I sat with them for almost an hour, such was their ridiculous notion of superiority over the staff and their two guests that I took great delight in insulting them at almost every juncture in the conversation. Only the two who had been kind to the waitress caught the true sense of my words, and if they were horrified, then they didn't show it. I ordered desserts all round, telling the waitress to go to the toilet first and make sure she didn't wash her hands. I passed her a fifty-euro note for her trouble and told my two friends to not eat anything else that came to the table.

People don't need pushing into turning a blind eye if they believe it is part of retribution for being made to feel insignificant. They just need a smile and a promise that you are looking out for them. The desserts came, a bountiful affair. I smiled at the waitress and congratulated her for having brought out such a specimen of delight. "My friends," I announced to the others at the table, "tuck in! You will not find a better taste than this. *Profiter, voici vos déserts juste!*" and I saluted them, imploring the other two to raise their glasses as well, which they did without hesitation and with extraordinary relish.

Out of the corner of my eye, I noticed the girl who had gone down the alley come crawling out, staggering to her feet and setting off unsteadily towards Rue Gabrielle. I made my humblest apologies to the crowded table. Catching the waitress washing her hands, I gave her another hundred euros and told her to make sure the two who had spoken to her kindly had no part in the bill, this was on me, and I enjoyed it immensely. She nodded, another moment in which a pawn becomes a queen. Pity it will cause her restaurant to close down, but never mind. I never liked the tea there.

I kept a discreet distance from the staggering girl, she looked as if she had got away with her life. I watched as people tried to avoid her, crossing the street when the traffic allowed, standing firm, almost motionless, a still wind that would not pick up the scent of frustrated decay. I doubt she saw anyone; she may have thought she was truly alone in this world, and whilst I deplore the anxieties of weak people, weak women especially, I was transfixed by this girl. I followed her for some distance, avoiding her sight, staying in the shadows, keeping away from the police who didn't move to stop her, not concerned with yet another party girl fallen sour of her date: move along, keep moving.

Finally, she came to some steps that led to the Seine, and she stood there gazing into its nighttime sleep-filled dreams. She was entranced, as if an ornate mirror had been placed before her, and was startled into making words of admiring beauty rather than focusing on the dreadful, emaciated state she was in.

For the first time in my life when it came to an unknown woman, I reached out to her and bade her *salam*. It was enough to turn her head, enough to make her stand there for a while, unsure of the action she should now take. I think she had intended to drown herself, to be perhaps immortalised like Roy Lichtenstein's *Secret Hearts*, to be a pop-culture icon for the newspapers and magazines. Perhaps then her boyfriend—or girlfriend; what did I care?—would be forever devastated, using the experience to seek a way out of the eternal blackness they faced. I am nothing but a businessman with one eye always open to a potential market.

The rest is history, or is it maybe my future? Somewhere over the Atlantic, we hit turbulence, and amongst the sudden shouts of surprise and the quick conversions to religion, I lean back in my seat and look longingly at the menu.

From the opening moment in which I spoke to her—not initially to save her life, but I like to think just to prolong it for a while so I could hear for myself her tale of woe—I felt a sense of duty to the girl, and when I found out who her father was, I could not help myself for having the intuition to follow her. I am a believer in such things. It is why I am still alive, despite the setbacks, despite how many of my people have suffered at the hands of dictators, presidents and soldiers looking to earn a medal or two.

I became her best friend; in turn, she became something else. I settled her debt, I gave her responsibility, and I made sure she graduated. Now I will make sure she stays in Paris with me and behaves as she should. If that means seeing her sister out of the equation, then so be it.

I wonder if she remembers the area where I dropped her off before making my way to Charles de Gaulle Airport. I doubt she would even think back to that time when she could have had her throat slit in some back alley close to Montmartre, where the smell of urine and cat shit mingle freely in the air and add to the Parisian fragrance in which so many profess their love under the stars and in view of the Eiffel Tower. As she sits there, her pencil skirt and matching hat giving the impression of elegance, does she think of the way her life almost ended, and who saved her with a simple gesture, seeing not some jilted Ophelia racked with guilt over her plight but a siren looking for a home?

Does she think about home? Does she imagine someday that she will return to the city of her birth and claim it as if it were second prize in a lottery draw? She is ambitious; she knows how to handle the best of society and the very dregs of civilisation. The poor and the addicted, the obscenely rich abuser and the burned-out junkie all have their price in my world.

As we approach New York I set out my plan. As always, I can see it so clearly, rarely beaten, always crystal clear. I love New York, I don't spend enough time here. One day, I shall come back when the need is not so pressing; it seems a long time since I have found amusement. How I miss the days when I could see a waitress give her customers a good bout of gastroenteritis.

John F. Kennedy, what a guy—a personal hero of mine. Despite his apparent illnesses, you just have to see the way he held himself so stiffly. Despite his fuck of a father, he still managed to seduce one of the most beautiful women on Earth and marry one of the most alluring. Good for him, pleased that he had an airport named after him—a far better name than that stuffed-up general whom Paris favours anyway. It is like a city in itself, full of the desperate, the hopeful and the borrowed, all looking for their entrance to the dream, their bite of the Big Apple not offered by an old witch dressed in black but a fair maiden holding a torch in one hand and a Calville Blanc d'hiver in the other, licking her lips as the economy of the nation bites back hard on its working-class souls.

The secret of getting through the tough regiment of border and passport control is to act as if you belong, and I do not need permission to belong anywhere. A young man with an oversize khaki rucksack adorned with a recently stitched on British flag barges past me, excited at what will be the time of his life as a young woman who has no doubt waited patiently opens her arms and screams his name. I hate the falseness but as he turns to apologise to me for almost knocking me over, I wave him off with a smile and a salutation: "*Espérons qu'elle vous donne le clap.*" He squints at me and asks what I said. "Forgive me," I reply. "I hope she says yes, you both deserve a clap, an applause for being so in love."

His smile broadens and he gives me a thumbs up. I wink at him and turn my attention to getting to the departure lounge. I want to find the best vantage point from which to see the object of my affections turn up and scout out her safe place before she meets her sister. I already told Catherine where the best place is, but like so many of her generation, she knows better.

I take my phone out of my pocket as I walk, cumbersome things but useful these days, and I dial the number of a man I know in Cleveland. He put me in touch with a couple of men. My own luck is holding: for whatever reason they are already in Cleveland, having gone there a few days beforehand to help a friend get across the border. I ask them how much it will be to do a simple job. A price is always agreeable when you let those in your employ dictate it. They don't get greedy, and if they do, they don't get to talk about it with someone else afterwards.

I ask why they are still there. Will it not raise suspicions once they drop off their cargo? The one doing the majority of the talking says something in his own language. I hate that I don't understand; I despise it when someone else laughs at a joke I don't get.

I let it go. After all, I need them to pay a discreet visit on someone. I give them the address and sign off, content that by the end of the day two outstanding concerns will have been erased.

Contrary to popular belief, the counterculture never went away, it just became franchised. We live in a world where those who tuned out now run empires. Every concession stand, every bit of tat for sale at a reasonable price, no matter where you go, no matter who you do with business with—it all comes down to the weight of expectancy and currency. I order a cup of coffee, feeling nauseous at the groping sense of human pursuit as people wave goodbye before returning to their cars driven on stolen oil, making time for everything but truth. I choose a spot in the middle of it all, smiling, wishing for a disease to take them. A cup of coffee slowly cooling in my hand, I spot her, frightened but not alone.

Chapter Fourteen

Chain Letter

The Detective

I DON'T SPEND MUCH time at the airport, not that I don't have the occasional need to be up there on official business. I just find the whole experience to be a chore, especially as I don't leave the island all that often, and when I do, I prefer to travel by boat and then by rail. That, of course, eats into the time I have available for enjoying a holiday or a trip abroad.

The last time I was up here was when I came back from meeting Aakster's parents and then being their guest at an award ceremony in which my friend was afforded a wonderful accolade arranged by her father in the wake of her participation in bringing down Marshall Rhagodidae.

Aakster had once told me that we are all connected by a common thread, one individual who, for good or for ill, has touched all our lives in some way, that friend of a friend behind the scenes pulling a string and watching our marionette-sculpted fleshy crawling bodies respond. Her family had suffered at the hands of that evil, as had mine and countless others around the world; by a common thread we all hanged.

I had time to kill. My chief had arrived at the hospital in a timely fashion and with news of events earlier in the day. They had charged Capone with attempted murder on the understanding that it would be increased if Corrish were to die because of his injuries. That was something, at least. As to the scorpion in our camp, the chief was none the wiser. There were a couple of whispers, of course. Senior men, trusted by the chief and not involved with the previous administration, had made discreet enquiries and a couple of names had been bandied around, but it was just supposition, hearsay and conjecture, no hard facts. For my own gut, I trusted only the chief and myself, but even we could fall foul of our position given the right shove.

The chief was accompanied by the duty desk sergeant Melina Borg. I was not surprised to see her. A warm heart prone to taking the job personally, not being able to walk away, she looked exhausted. I assumed he had brought her to keep her mind off the events of the attack, given it had happened on her watch.

They were going to take turns to guard Corrish, a wise move for sure. I would have given good odds against anyone tackling Melina Borg and coming away with less than a black eye and wounded male pride; the rugby team was lucky to have her.

The chief instructed me to take a couple of hours for myself before heading up to the airport and collecting our English visitor. "Take time to think, my friend," he told me and clapped me on the back.

I could have gone anywhere; I certainly could have gone home for an hour, put on a fresh shirt, eaten a sandwich, listened to one of those vinyl albums I had purchased a couple of weeks ago but remained in the box in which they had been delivered. I kept meaning to put them away, but like everything else, I found I didn't want to forget their meaning so quickly—replacements for the ones broken by my ex-wife in a fit of spite when we divorced.

So yes, there was any number of places I could have gone, but somehow, I ended up at the airport, arriving by bus, plenty of baggage surrounding me, weighing me down, thankful I didn't have to pay an excess charge as I marched purposefully towards the arrivals board to check the plane was still on time and then made my way to the small coffee bar on the side of the building and ordered a drink.

I remember when this terminal opened. I was on duty, as was my father, although his responsibility was greater than mine. He was also a bookended presence, requested to oversee the transition of our island in joining a larger community: more visitors equals more potential for crime to visit our shores. He had been on duty when the old terminal was the scene of the island's more recent spotlights in the news.

I looked around those sampling one last drink before their flights home, the children already bored and wanting to head back to the beach, their parents frazzled by the unexpected delay and wishing they had booked more than just a few days away. I imagined the bustle and concern, the sheer terror and panic that had swept across the island back in my father's heyday, when the hijacking of planes almost reached ritualistic proportions across Europe.

My father, cool, calm, and one who had the ear of those in power on the island, had advised the then prime minister when Flight 861 had been hijacked en route from Amsterdam to Tokyo, and he was involved again as a liaison when Flight 616 was hijacked in 1985. He took that one personally; we all do in a way, so many dead on our land, caught as we are between Europe and Africa, the old colonial system ever-present in those dominating three colours, the sometimes distrusted view of Europe and the old kings, the African coastline with its images of exotic dusk and sand that comes and hits our shores when the wind is high and in the wrong direction.

I turned my head away from the scene unfolding in my mind. This was perhaps the real reason I never came up here, why I always preferred taking the long way around, a relaxing journey by sea. Even then, ghosts of the island found ways to haunt me, not fully letting go until I had landed on the coast of Sicily. Too often did I look over the side of the boat and see my sister floating in the sea, forever drowning, always just a girl, trying to impress a boy.

I stood and stretched out my arms as if to make a show of feeling the tension release; such memories were no good for the soul.

So much had been inflicted upon our island, it was hard not to take it all personally. Recent events had caused grief that drove a wedge between our government and the people. The thin line had been crossed: a car bomb, the constant building of ever-taller apartment buildings which our young could not afford but were a wealth magnet for those who had no interest in the true passion of the island. We'd had our moments in history's shame, the political football that had been kicked around between empires, and we'd had moments of greatness, when the world looked upon our shores with hope that the Cold War was over. It was a moment of great pride when the summit between Russia and America happened in our home—even for me, as young man still reeling from my actions that put a small black mark in my father's books. I had shaken the hands of a couple of the American delegation, those on the fringes of history.

We are all participants in history's wake. Our input into what makes the world go around is up to us, but we are all connected. What affects you soon troubles me, a plague of thoughts and counter-decisions always biting down on our minds as we make our way along Time's path.

How long I stood there I don't know, but an older woman carrying an oversize bear in one arm and a pile of chocolate in the other asked if I was using the table or just taking up space in the hope of attracting conversation. I flashed her my warrant card and told her I was watching a suspect who was a known bag-snatcher and pickpocket. Her tone had been one of arsenic-driven entitlement, so I kicked back and used my authority to make her feel small, which was not in my nature. I apologised and asked her if she wanted a coffee or a cold drink perhaps. It was a connection; we are all joined by the same thread. Had I not rectified my position immediately, she would have gone on to be snide to someone else, and so the chain continues.

I walked back to the bar and brought her a cold drink. For good measure, I threw in a sandwich. Upon returning, I told her what I had ordered: if she didn't want it then no offence at all, just ask for a different one and they would change it. She seemed thankful, and then she started to cry. She had come to Malta to meet a grandchild she had never seen, but the baby's mother— her daughter-in-law—refused to let her visit, telling her she had no rights. The trip had all been arranged before her son's death, and this was supposed to reconnect her to the family she had left. I felt bad for her, annoyed at a system that allowed this to go on. There was nothing, however, that I could do. I do not make the law; I only observe it happening.

I sat with her for half an hour, listening, taking in the tale, and it made me think of my son who had refused to have anything to do with me since his mother died at the hands of her lover— a man who had also wanted me dead.

We talked until she looked at her watch and declared she needed to get to the departure lounge. We shook hands, and I was thankful that in some way I managed to preserve a chain and not set fire to it. It was a small act, one which began with my being authoritarian, high and mighty, and caught out by my resurrected memories.

I said goodbye and mimicked her watch-checking: almost perfect timing; the evidence of Corrish's life would soon be here. I looked down at my phone and found the photograph that this woman who held a man's life in her hands had sent to me, not for the first time thinking she didn't look a bit how I imagined any member of the clergy to be.

I had a lot of questions for Mrs. Dymek, but I was more intrigued to meet the woman who caused Ms. Corrish to be particularly vile. Her photo, probably taken that day as she headed to the airport, showed a woman with a lot on her mind, and despite appearing to be the kind one might expect to see on the cover of a fashion magazine, there was a homely quality to her that I found endearing. She had already told me a little of herself, perhaps thinking a forewarning might avoid later awkwardness of mistaking friendliness for sexual interest, as certain men are wont to do. She need not have worried on that score; I felt sure my days of being attracted to anyone were long since dead.

I watched the board tick over and was grateful to see that the plane had landed safely. I had already asked the chief to contact the powers-that-be at the airport to ensure she was met personally and whisked through security with as little fuss as possible. There was no large suitcase to collect; all she had was a bag containing enough clothes for a couple of days. When I had texted her before she got on the plane and asked her what she would be carrying, all she said was hope. I don't know if hope needs searching, placing on a roller and then scanning electronically. It amused me slightly to believe it did. After all, we might then see what would flag up as false faith before it took flight and spread promises it could not keep.

Twenty minutes passed; I was concerned. Then she appeared, holding the hand of an elderly man who was being pushed in a wheelchair by one of the airport staff. She saw me waiting and waved apologetically, beckoning for me to come and help her. There was a young man waiting not far from me who also caught sight of the wave and rushed over as if he had been granted one last chance of redemption. He fell upon the older gentleman and gave him the warmest of hugs, a tender moment which is always priceless to witness.

As I approached the small party of strangers, the younger man was shaking Mrs. Dymek's hand with enthusiasm and gratefulness. She smiled at me and introduced me to the two men, father and son. The father had flown to Malta after many years away, coming back to spend his last years with his family. He had left his wife and son when the younger was but a child, terrified of the responsibility. Mrs. Dymek had kept him company during the flight—I got the feeling she had acted as a kind of confessor, listening to the old man's concerns without judgement. Again, I thought of my son. Somewhere out there, possibly even close by, was my blood, my lad, and I felt ashamed.

Leaving the old man in the safe arms of his son, we walked away from the scene of happiness. Out of the corner of my eye, I studied her, taking in her full height, her gait, the air of humility and warmth I had just witnessed. It was impossible not to like her…and to see why Ms. Corrish felt such antagonism towards her.

I took her solitary bag, light as a baby's conscience, and told her we would get a taxi to the station where we could discuss the situation in private. Then I would get her to the hospital so she could sit with her friend for as long as she needed. She thanked me and stopped for a moment, undoing the mark of her calling from around her neck. Noticing my quizzical frown, she laughed and explained she was not at work now. She was here to help her friend and me in any way she could.

It was a moment that broke any ice that might have lingered between us. I realised she had not been anything other than a counsel for other people's problems for some time, and whilst she was frightfully afraid for her friend, she could now just be that: a friend; not some spiritual guide and held-aloft member of the community. She could just be Rose Dymek.

In the evening air, I turned to look back at the airport, watching families wide-eyed in wonder at the adventure to come as they explored the beauty my island had to offer. I hoped they would find a little piece of heaven that they could share and talk of forever. It was a good place, a country where sometimes bad things happened, just the same as everywhere else. It was the people that made it work.

We walked to the taxi, and I opened the door for her, breathing in the sense of freedom my chief had afforded me for the last couple of hours. I could have gone home, played records, shaved and worried whether the ham in the fridge was on the turn. I could have taken a taxi down to St. Julian's Bay for a while or even returned to my once-shared den of drunken release in Valletta. Instead, I had come to a place I usually avoided. I may not have boarded a plane today, but I had travelled a great distance. I had begun my journey back to being a member of the island community rather than just enforcing its laws and clearing up after dead men's lies.

Climbing into the other side of the taxi, I told the driver where we needed to go. Along the way, I pointed out a couple of local interests, making a mental note that if she had the time, I would happily show this considerate woman around the island, no longer mine, but a place where all could come.

Chapter Fifteen

To Feel Nothing and See Everything at the Same Time

Corrish Underwater

*I*CAN HEAR THEM *shout my name in concern as I disappear from view, only to break out in laughter and the odd expletive of damnation when I rupture through the water's crest and stand between them, the forgotten summer ones few care for whilst they stay on the beach, surrounded by the confidence of youth, and the damage that needed to rectified by a new system of belief. I am back with them. How is that possible? It has been nearly thirty years since I let the Atlantic waves splash against my face, since I sat reading poetry on these American beaches and smoked until my mind was raw and willing to accept a new reality.*

We are the desperate, the nihilistic, the product of the revolution that failed when we needed it most. We languish in our decline as the sun beats down and leaves us exhausted and emotionless, then races off to find the rescued of San Francisco and the spiritual chanting reflected in the dawn of eager faces in a land which saw two suns rise one August day in 1945, circling stars inflating, pushing out their seed as if in the last throes of enforced and guilt-ridden labour, the dance of the dead now celebrated every day; as those who lived mourn, we find that we come alive and join them.

The bonfire on the beach has been alight for days, perhaps weeks now. Time is a blur. I have smoked and drunk myself to the point of oblivion so many times I have become the reflecting sonnet-bearer, the zombie granted the kind of immortality only ever intended for Jim Morrison. As more skin falls off me, more is revealed underneath, forever renewing. I am sick, and I have enjoyed the destruction I have brought upon myself.

I hear the ticking of a clock close by, but I am still in the water and have not worn a watch for months now. Then I remember there is a clock tower that stands on the sidewalk just past the beach and through the wafts of white smoke and the distant smell of corndogs burning on the bonfire, I watch the face of the clock at a standstill. Time to relive it all again.

Relive what, exactly? I was in a holding area—hold on to that thought, it is important, do not lose sight of where you really are.

If the shores of Northern Ontario were my haven, then this is my hell, and I relish it. I want to get lost; I want to experience the pressure of the true revolution, right here in the ocean, on the beach. I want to impale my heart and my guts and offer them as a renegade donation to the gods, and then I want to sit against the rock I have claimed as my own and eat, smoke and drink, make jokes, laugh at the rotten core of humanity, empathise with stories of hardship and pain, and of the beauty of madness as it embraces each one of us. We are all infected by the waste of our time. Such insanity. The only sane thing to do is to forget.

I am grabbed by the arm, my new friends pulling me towards the shore. Our madness is infectious, yet we do nothing to cause concern amongst the locals. We keep the beach clean; we look after the children when the parents want to swim; we have our own commune here in the circle of hell, and yet we are the good guys.

There are more joining us this weekend. Some out-of-towners, not refugees like me. Not misplaced effigies of our former selves, just friends of friends who are coming from New York and Washington for a grand old party that is not ignorant of all the shit that comes with being consumed.

And we have been consumed. We have been opened up and had our souls stolen, harvested, pocketed, with no chance of receiving any type of reimbursement. Come as you are, roll up, roll up, a perfect gift for Christmas. Cost, my dear? Just a mountain of debt, fear, the worry of sexual diseases. Hey, after all, you lived through the Cold War and celebrated when the Berlin Wall came down, but remember we also brought you the beast of Chernobyl, the trouble with borders and national tensions, the ease of breathing in dragon fumes, bombs, bombs, bombs, always being dropped...

I am thirsty and allow myself to be picked up out of the water by a girl who is stronger than me, and we laugh as she runs to the group half-asleep by the bonfire, shouting, "I saved Ash! He nearly drowned!"

The clock tower is louder here, I can barely hear myself think as I dry myself off and notice how thin I have become. Several months have passed since I last ate a huge meal: my friends in Pittsburgh had reserved a table at one of the best restaurants in town the night before I said I should be on my way, enough with the rivers, I need to see the land again...I am waving to the ships on the distant horizon, and yet it is me who is drowning.

Names mentioned are greeted with a cheer. I don't know who they are, but then I didn't know this group of college kids before I got here. I arrived intending to stay for a couple of days; in my mind, I wanted to head to the other ocean; I wanted to walk towards the glowing sunset. Instead, I stayed here, enticed by others who wanted me to be open, to see my shadow burn itself onto the stones behind, a timeless memorial to the two suns we have come to worship.

These are the people coming to join us, and I smile at the thought of the party that might ensue. I still have some money left, enough for one last rage on the beach, then perhaps I will have to start my journey back across the States and take a job or two along the way. The consumption of my soul is beginning again in earnest. The fire is bright, it crackles with heat, our source of fuel almost running out; I close my eyes and dream.

***

The group therapy sessions drag on, urging us to talk about our feelings. I swear I left such emotions behind in one last drunken orgy on the beach. The counsellor tells me my attitude is not helpful. Her quiet demeanour and laid-back approach to ridiculing us is that of a teacher who has been told by the headmaster that she can no longer throw chalkboard erasers at our heads and who now contemplates how the game of dodgeball could benefit him in asserting power over those in his dominion.

She crosses her arms and looks at me in defiance. I hate her. All I want to do is ignore her, to ring my mum or Rose to get me out of this hell hole, starched white and clean, the physical reminder of purity and relentless obsessive dusting, but there are cracks in the foundations. Dust occasionally crawls out on the backs of invisible insects, the occasional wobble of gangly legs performing the ritual of spreading disease, our generation's disease and floundering passion for The Programme.

The room may look white, but outside these four walls, there are signs of the badly maintained, the odd scar of mildew, moss in the guttering, poison ivy that from a distance looks charming and in character when it is pulling at the fabric of our reality. We will all die in here, as the building collapses around us, brick and plaster dust infecting our lungs until, finally, that hard smack on the head which brings us to our senses...and all the while the counsellor's watch is ticking, marking time, get in order, fall in line and be responsible consumers.

I came here to stop the need. I had fallen on bad habits the final year of university. I found I was thinking of someone I could not quite place, a girl's face lost in the murky remains of excuses and the crackdown imposed on me by...by...Annalise.

***

"You will enter yourself into the programme and stop being so selfish. Don't you think you have caused enough trouble..."

Her teeth, I had never noticed how big my sister's teeth were, shark grin, clamping down on the helpless seal...or the human being who resembled it. Food is food at the end of the day. That was it. I was always food to Annalise, we all were.

Devoured, spat out, regurgitated, sister knows best, the whole village despising her, terrified of her as she swam in circles, the bait set, patiently waiting for the struggle to end, then pounce, tearing skin from bone, ripping apart hope, searing its dominance on its territory, all over in seconds. Digested and somehow returned to life only to experience it again and again. Until you can face it no more, swim away...

I swam away. I heard the clock ticking and my heart grew tired. I was about to be a meal again...

***

I had been lonely for years. My best friend warned me that my ex-wife was just another version of Annalise, but sitting in her living room, empty whisky bottles strewn across the floor, taken down by the bowling ball of her logic, the direct hit earning the coveted X on the first throw, I stared at my friend and her wife and knew I had failed to outswim Annalise. I had nothing, just regrets. I should have stayed looking out from a Canadian shore. I should have not come home, not married, not been alive...and the clock keeps ticking.

***

The final party, how glorious it had been. There must have been around three hundred of us there, a mini Woodstock, happy that we had survived until now. The call of adulthood was upon us. I wanted to carry on travelling, but I was urged over a can of beer to go back home and study—"You can always come back, dude." I took a drag of her cigarette and told her she was crazy. She may be willing to sell her soul in pursuit of a big house, expensive cars and clothes that had come with a price that made my eyes sore just to think of it. But me? No way. I was a free spirit, not tied to a clock...just an open road and two suns in the dawn to keep me company. She laughed and offered me a tablet. "Let's go down the route together, sunshine. Let's see who wins."

*The townspeople who had witnessed our continued existence on the beach had become our friends. On occasion, a cop tried to throw his weight around but was met with polite resistance. No major laws were broken; some of us even worked during the day. None of us were vagrants, and we kept the music down low. Sometimes I preferred the solitude of my Walkman, the music of The Doors, Marillion, Genesis…early morning Manhattan…wait, what…why am I thinking of there now? No, let's stay here…let's stay on the beach…think, what else did I listen to? Music was always my constant companion, on this trip especially…*come as you are…as a friend…

The bonfire was the largest we had built the whole time we had made the beach our home. Those with trucks had scouted down as much wood as they could carry, one even going all the way down the Jersey shoreline and bringing back the remains of a couple of trees that had washed ashore down by Benny's Landing. We had drink, there was conversation, there was music…there was a face looking at me quizzically through the haze and heat of the fire. She was holding a man's hand and noticed I had seen her spying on me, examining my face, scanning for recollection. She turned away… the clock tower striking seven with precision. I felt a nudge in my side, and a young man asked if I was happy, placing his hand on my knee as he did so. I politely smiled but told him I was not interested in what he was suggesting. He took it well and winked at another man about our age who had come with the others from New York. I raised a toast to his health, then he was gone.

So too was the face from across the bonfire. I stood and walked gingerly around to where I thought she had been sitting. The tablet I had taken was working its way through my system, and I felt a giggle well up inside me. I shouted to those sharing this final encounter in the shadow of two suns that we are the madness that keeps our generation afloat and grounded. We are the disposed, the unwanted, the nihilistic and the groundbreakers of our own decline. They cheered and threw caution to the wind, carried alongside the ashes of dead trees.

There was a space in the crowd…

Why was there a space? I put my earphones back over my head and listened to whatever song was ready to become part of the moment. I saw a police boat hugging the shoreline, ready to stop anyone going out too far, and then I bumped into her...she was there...she was there. I could not believe it. I spoke her name, but she ignored me. I touched her shoulder and got ready to say hello, but as she turned around, something was different. There was cruelty in her tone, a withering sound of time that had once decayed. Now, instead of holding a hand and reconnecting, I was told to get off her.

I said her name slowly. She shook her head violently. My name is...my name is... She had said it with so much strength, but the sound of the clock tower drowned out her words. No, that's not right. I know I heard her name. The man who was with her pushed me back, telling me to stop bothering his wife. "I wasn't bothering. I have never been that type of man. You want bothering, you should meet my sister Annalise."

He pushed me again, but I knew it was her. I put up my hands and opened them. I was doing my best to subdue the tension, but when I looked down at his shirt pocket, there was a tape cassette inside it, half exposed, giving his chest an odd robotic edge, a flaw...
come as you are...as a fiend...

I staggered back. I felt like I had been punched in the gut. My abdomen hurt, yet he hadn't laid a fist on me. I turned around, confused, and wandered off towards the ocean. Several of my friends had noticed the situation: one of them called out to me to forget it; another asked who the hell they thought they were, this couple of outsiders. Had they even been invited? Bad form to mess with a friend...come back, Ash, forget it. Forget it, man.

I made my way to the water's edge. I felt anger in me and wanted to punch out. I had taken so much abuse from my sister. I had left my home in search of meaning, and now...the water beckoned me...
come as you are...so I did.

***

You hit that counsellor once, why did you not hit the man who pushed you? Different moments, different reactions. The counsellor was peddling drugs into the facility; we were her lab rats. This man...what had he done except protect his wife?

***

I heard footsteps running on the sand, but I continued to walk into the sea. I took off my earphones and wound them around the Walkman, the soundtrack of my life now dead. My soles were just touching the sand; another inch and I would be swept off my feet. I hurled my Walkman into the air as the anger finally released itself, and I watched it fall as Icarus had fallen...as I was about to fall. It landed with a thud on the police boat's windscreen, and in that singular action, I heard the splintering of my time.

My friend's voice urged me to come back to the bonfire, everybody would claim it was one of the jumbucks who had stayed away from the group, preferring instead to race around the town in stolen vehicles and shooting tyres. I shouted to the dying sun to come and take me home. Here I am, nothing is real in this plastic paradise.

My friend asked the two who they were. I didn't hear his first name, but she introduced herself as Abigael Wells, and they had come down from New York City that afternoon. "Well, Abigael Wells, fuck back off to New York before you get into any trouble here. I'll tell them that you started this." My friend was pointing at the police boat that was coming closer.

My body ached. It was beginning to bruise, but my eyes were closing. I felt like I had been repeatedly punched, kicked in the head...the police are coming now, no time to run, it's over.

My friend screamed at me. Others joined in, those I had spent so much time with all shouting in unison, "Wake up. You need to wake up now. Tick, tick, tick...Abigael Wells..."

Wake Up!

Chapter Sixteen

The Apparent Death of Samantha Ó Foghladh

(Part One)

T HE PROBLEM WITH the close-up assassination is that nobody really cares about the drama unless they happen to be paying very close attention to how it panned out from start to finish, especially when the person doesn't die straight away and their death is prolonged over the course of several minutes, an hour, days even.

It is in the anticipation that the playful assassin will get their kicks, a stage in which we excel. Not for us, the gunshot from a distance, hiding behind the slats of a window pulled across to cast a small nefarious shadow when the sun positions itself just right. The killer gets the full-page story; the assassin, we just get the headline.

I'm not averse to slowing down my breathing, being patient, taking my time to deliver the bite at exactly the right moment, my fingers poised, my heart rate escalating to the point where the release of the bullet is every bit as momentous as the final throes of sex when both participants have had their fill.

Now is not the time for a carefully placed bullet; not the place for a drama. If I shoot her, someone will see.

No, I want to watch the pain unfold. I want to sit and drink a cup of America's version of coffee, perhaps munch my way through a pastry or a family-size packet of chips. I want to be entertained by the suspense of waiting for her to take a sip of the drink and then carry on her business as if nothing has happened...until suddenly the curtain comes down and there is no encore for the crowd; always leave them wanting more.

There is drama and then there is theatre. A drama will have the crowds scattering, running haphazardly, but people fall over left-behind suitcases, someone could get hurt. A drama can unfold as if it is scripted—I can almost see the writer toying with the idea for the screen, the vantage point found, the expression of quiet etched upon the killer' face, his moral anguish quelled by the thought of a payday. We don't know his back story yet; perhaps he does it to raise cash for his daughter who desperately needs a life-saving operation, or perhaps he does it because the government have got to him, figures in suits, smiles of fake sincerity as they promise it is just a one-time thing. *Do this for us and we will take care of your daughter. If you get caught, know she will be safe.*

Drama has its place, but theatre, now *that* is the true passion of the artist. Seen but not seen, at the side of the stage feeding the best lines to the main actor, watching the female lead shine gloriously in the limelight as she brings courage in death to the part, being someone else for a while, an Ophelia for the times, the Lady Macbeth revealing her sadism and using the excuse to partake in murder...ahh, the theatre of it all. A film will explain everything; theatre can be shrouded in darkness, for there is no rewind on the stage. A line whispered from the understudy in the wings can bring a different effect every night, and the crowd below go wild with applause.

I know a hundred ways to kill a person, from the quick release of the broken neck to the gunshot to the heart, it may seem like boasting and an easy way to rid yourself of a problem, but they are effective. They just lack true style.

There is so much to see here, people being greeted by the second, a million stories being relayed, all this connection.

It is enough to bring a tear to the eye and a lump to the throat. I had better go and order a meal; I feel like steak.

Dear Samantha, I have heard so much about you, and there you are, less than twenty metres away from me. I could introduce myself, that would be fun. It's not likely you will remember in an hour or two anyway. Slumped over in a chair, just another heart failure, a statistic for the airport authorities to include in their yearly reports.

You are nothing like your sister, not physically. Smaller, more than eight or nine centimetres shorter. Your hair colour is different, and the way you hold yourself in public… Your sister, even at her lowest ebb, still held herself with a kind of regal outlook. She was a queen in waiting, while you… As I watch you scanning the people milling around you for a face you might know, I see nothing more than a maid, a serving girl, a wretch—you remind me of the lost children found by Fagin but washed and presented to the world as if you are something special instead of the personification of a vagabond—what is that quaint term used in the British Midlands? Oh, yes. A wench. Samantha, you are a wench.

But you are not alone. Beside you is a young man, good-looking in an offbeat way, his eyes sparkling, deep, as if they had just had the allusion of Belladonna added to them, the illusion loved by so many women in the Middle Ages. Let in the light, dear boy. It is as good a poison as any.

Poison: the choice of the female murderer, so people would have you believe. I have often thought about that. I suspect a woman can use it without having to look into their victim's eyes, a sense of distance, easier to maintain innocence. A man will do the same with a bullet or a bomb, but when it comes to the personal, strangulation seems to be the most effective. For that, you have to be part of the dance, you have to lead, to step out of the shadows that surround the stage and announce yourself to the audience. The crowd, seeing your face, make a note in their programme of your performance. Too many critics these days are ready to give a review that doesn't match your interpretation of the part you played.

Women have the best role in death, especially when they are the ones inflicting the pain. With a man, it becomes immediate and personal; it is the uncontrollable anger like an orgasm gone wrong, full of black wrath, an inky, foul-smelling substance that comes. Even in the hands of the assassin, it is still a projectile that delivers the fatal blow. Of course, I know a couple of women who can tear themselves off emotionally, look down the sight of a gun and kill a person without blinking. Then there are those who harness the same rage of the moment but use a knife to the gut—homoerotic in a way, twisting it, getting their hands bloodied. I applaud that.

But for the woman who has been given time, who has let their resentment fester, the cold, calculating heart is one I admire the most. If you want to bring down society, if you want to see a civilisation fall, don't use a man; find a woman with a long-held grudge and hate in her heart. It worked for those in charge of Belsen.

The man beside Samantha is of no consequence. If anything, it is an added bonus to have a star witness, and by the time they realise all is lost, I shall be back in my Paris apartment. I might even be in time to pick up a phone call from a devastated Catherine, the understudy urging the leading lady to let out the pain. Too late to save Ophelia, Gertrude will carry the consequences of another's actions with her for all time, damned as the court around her crumbles.

So, who are you, my beautiful boy holding Ophelia's hand? It is all a little too tender but new, isn't it? Did she find you along the way? Is this real for you, or are you just playing the hero, the shoulder to cry on in the hope of having her lean on you more than she realises? I can understand that; it is business, is it not? Do you think you are the lead in this production? Surely not.

Like me, you are the one to whom no credit will be forthcoming, just a passage in which the heroine of the piece is able to have someone close by as she fills the page with tears and regret, and all before yielding to the inevitability of the final act. *Son père confesseur?* Perhaps I'll have to deal with you at the same time. Perhaps not. It could work that you are just the observer, the waiter at the Last Supper who described in detail all he had seen and could not be discreet about Jesus and Mary as the wine went to their heads.

Catherine would only be an hour or so behind me, the age of constant travel always leaving its mark on the sky above us. So many people aboard a flying bomb, a weapon of war that carries civilians as its cargo. It was a lesson I learned when I read up on the history of hijacking—a cumbersome and costly affair, but effective if used in the right scenario. Not my style, though. Again, it is like the bomb. Too much drama and not enough theatre.

Is that how that boy we found on the boat would have described it? The one who caused me to lie low while others took my place. Theatre is easy if you find the right understudy to take the role of the one in the spotlight.

Time to get this performance started.

Getting a clear liquid through customs is easy. I hate alcohol myself, but vodka is a perfect solution in which a vial of one poison can easily replace another, and I always found it necessary to keep such bottles to hand. There is a distinct craft to the art of poison: too much and the effect can be spoiled by too much drama. The film industry has a lot to answer for, raising the expectations of those seeking the quick thrill. It is what those animals at Treblinka, Auschwitz and Belzec aspired to, greedy fuckers. Not that I have any particular love for the Jews, but such an action—you will not convince me it is anything other than a horrific waste, the sexual fantasies of a mad man.

I feel inside my left pocket, the glass of the bottle seemingly warm against my fingers, or is it just the eager anticipation of the understudy in the wings, nervous for the line he has to deliver, understanding that the way he pronounces to the audiences will see the play progress favourably? I am excited, time ticking away, and if I'm right with my timing then Gertrude will find her Ophelia starting her journey downstream, hands clasped in prayer as she silently leaves this world.

I take a small black leather holder from my carry case and make a show of pretending to take a reading of my sugar levels, ensuring I am seen but not observed. It is funny how many people will turn their heads away from someone performing this simple task. No one asks if I am all right; no one cares in this rush, this madness into which we throw ourselves headlong. I am just a man who is doing his best to avoid falling into a diabetic coma.

A group of people briefly shroud my view of Samantha and her male companion, but not so much that I can't see them waiting there on the two chairs, looking concerned. Frightened, perhaps. Do they know they are about to meet the devil, this Spider?

I stand and affect weariness. Ten feet away from my quarry; five feet and I start to slur my words slightly. I make eye contact with them both, I say my line, and they carry the scene to its conclusion. I sit between them and point to my bag. I tell them my syringe is already there—"Can you get me a drink please?" to which the boy gets up and leaves me alone with Samantha.

As she carefully scurries through my bag, I clutch her arm and fall forwards. She gives me a look of apprehension, of alarm, and asks if she can call anyone. Satisfied the needle coated in botulinum has scratched the skin of her forearm, I carry on the charade and tell her I will be all right in a few minutes. She tries to hand me the syringe, and I ask her to put it into my arm. A small touch of my own batch of medication, nothing that would show up too much in a drug test, not that I was expecting one. She doesn't show any signs of trepidation as she places the needle against my skin and presses downwards; by the time the boy comes back, I am happy to proceed and feeling euphoric. I drink the water and sit with them a while, thanking them both for their kindness, counting down the time until the poison takes effect. It will be quick, but the severity won't be felt for a few hours.

Having played my part, I stand and insist I'm feeling much better. Over the tops of people's heads, I see the information board change: the imminent arrival of the next inbound plane from Paris. I give them my thanks, even offering them some money so they can buy something to eat, but the girl shakes her head, so I bid them farewell and disappear into the crowd, melting away, feeling the slight touch of cocaine doing its job. I smile.

I walk back up the stairs to the balcony level and find a seat from which to witness stardom live forever as a public notice in some national newspaper. I wonder if my supporting role will be remarked upon, I feel I deserve, just this once, a nod to my creativity.

No matter what you think, it is not that hard to pull yourself away from a crime. After watching for a few minutes, I'm satisfied that I have done an excellent job, and that by the time Catherine finds her, Samantha will be feeling quite unwell. By the end of the day, she will be dead.

I whistle with a vigour I haven't experienced in quite some time. You can call a woman a whore as you laugh and they will fall in love with you, but it doesn't make you any happier. You can wish the clap on a man who barges past you in his rush to embrace the woman who came to meet him, but it only adds to the illusion of actively being in control. This, today, has been a return to form, and I feel alive.

I leave the arrivals terminal and casually make my way to departures. It's a long walk, but the flight home will be restful, and I have a couple of hours to kill.

**

My phone's ringing as I get out of the taxi outside my Paris address. It's Catherine, almost hysterical. She somehow got into a fight with her sister and caused her to collapse. In her panic, she left abruptly as calls for an ambulance were relayed across the concourse. How was she going to get home? Where had I been? She had been trying to call me for hours! I apologise, tell her I had business to take care of, but I will take care of it all. Where is she? I give her an address in New York City, a friend of mine who lives on 77th Street, just opposite the bar on the corner. Go there, I tell her. Wait until I call and all will be well.

Catherine has always been level-headed, cold and logical, but this is a nice turn of events in her make-up. She presented vulnerability, exhibited a concern for her safety that I have barely glimpsed in the years I have known her. I can use it to my advantage, to get her deeper into the nest.

All that matters for now is to phone my associate and tell him to expect a woman who will undoubtedly be flustered, in a panic, even in a rage. He snickers gruffly and says I could be describing any number of his girlfriends—"Hell, even my mother!"

I laugh heartedly. Today has been a good day—why should I not laugh? I tell him what I need him to do: provide Catherine with another false passport, burn the one in her possession and wait a couple of days before taking her to Newark Airport. There's a note of hesitation in his voice when he enquires what he's going to do with her for a couple of days. I laugh once again, and tell him anything he damn well pleases.

Chapter Seventeen

Rose Dymek's Letters

The Detective

THE LETTER WAS addressed to Ash, the blue *Par Avion* sticker on the front regimentally tight against the decades-old envelope, yet the words inside were still as cutting, as wounding and heartless as they had been when they were written nearly thirty years before. I turned off my mobile; I had already disconnected the office phone. This was not a time for interruptions, let the main desk take a message if needs be.

I smiled at Rose Dymek. The very act of bringing this and a number of other letters to my attention must have been one of love and friendship, not providing evidence to ensure justice was done. This felt like a favour being repaid, a long, outstanding debt wiped clean—or it could just be guilt from hiding the letters from Ash Corrish in the first place.

There were postcards, letters, hurriedly performed acts of cold communication, long moments of enthused correspondence, symbols and gestures. He had written occasionally, then at times with a flurry of news, several excited letters arriving over a matter of days. As I tried to piece them into some sort of order, the trail of Ash Corrish's thoughts came together and the scenes that had unfolded before him made sense to me.

Rose talked of times that were not documented: the time he was placed in care and the broken nose he gave the counsellor when she worked out she was placing her patients on illegal drugs;

the time when they were teenagers and they protected each other from the wrath of Ash's sister Annalise.

I looked up and away from the letters momentarily when she said, with a hint of damnation spiking every word, "She even snapped my Stranglers' tape in half."

I stared at Rose and raised both eyebrows. She didn't strike me as one to have got the punk scene, especially as she was about my age and a vicar raised in the English countryside.

"Punk and sandwiches for the village cricket team," I mused. "Surely life in the village was dull—wasn't that why Ash got out and why you left for university?" I generalised, knowing my words would be taken as gentle mocking and not some half-arsed attempt at provocation or masculine show of ignorance.

She smiled and told me she understood. It seemed there was more to Rose Dymek than met the eye. Her wife was a lucky woman. Both Ash and Rose had bonded over music: what Annalise had instilled through terror, fear and resentment, music had replaced with peace. Ash had followed the second wave of progressive rock and then later the American scene as he got to know his family history better, finding a connection with the words, with the violent angst.

Rose had instead found freedom in the punk scene, ten years out of date by then, and The Stranglers were her band of choice. I had to admit, amid the dispatches of the lone explorer, the missing pieces in the timeline of an innocent man, I found joy in her taste, remembering that in my new home there were several albums by the band and some others this strangely bohemian and firebranded member of the clergy might quite like to hear.

I lowered my head and continued reading. There were names Ash had already willingly given us, a couple of leads that had panned out and avenues of evidence that corroborated his story. Why had the American authorities been so keen to hang all this on Ash's head? Then there was this letter. I felt uneasy; everything else made sense. He talked of this girl having been so kind, so nice, it was almost as if he had been in love, but according to Rose, our mutual friend had fallen for women quite easily in his youth. These days, I got the feeling he would rather be left alone. I prayed that if he should recover, he might once again throw some caution to the wind and allow his heart to be bruised but also kissed soothingly by the same woman.

The letter had come within a couple of weeks of their initial meeting, smartly written but devoid of any personality save for the overwhelming appearance of cruelty. It also didn't read as if written by an American girl. It was sterile, infused with hatred— I had limited knowledge of such things, but I was sure something was missing. I re-read Ash's statement; there was mention of giving her a tape he had been carrying around. He had liked her enough to part company with something he had made.

Rose listened to my concerns, my first rummage out of the darkness, before explaining, "Before he left, he copied some of his albums onto tapes so he could have memories of home, the reasons to stay away. Each new place would then mean something else. Rather than being a song that reminded him of the time when Annalise beat him, it instead became the moment he went on the Staten Island ferry for the first time, or when he looked out across the New York City skyline with a group of friends from the hotel as they held hands and gave thanks to Lady Liberty.

"This was teenage stuff, the stuff of romance, not one that the writers of lonely housewife books would understand, but a boyish dream of running away, of being someone else whilst retaining just that one truth of yourself, the music that made you love in the first place."

There was no tape with the letter, nor even a mention of the tape. I asked Rose directly, and she shook her head in honest confusion. All that had come was the letter, so curt and terrible that she had never been able to show it to her friend. It had arrived at the university; she had read it, in case it was urgent, and been so shocked that she had kept it secret.

I asked her, "If you hated someone as much as the letter to Ash implies, would you not send back everything—every gift, no matter how small—they had given you to tell them to stay out of your life?"

She mused for a while before regaling me with an example. She had been seeing a fellow student at university, only to realise that the woman had been lying about her faith—something Rose had found unacceptable—and she returned a watch, cheap but adorable, the woman had given her. They had done that face-to-face, though; she was not one for writing 'Dear Joan' letters.

Again, I smiled, but I got to the point. If this Samantha had hated him as much as she declared in the letter, surely she would have mentioned the tape. She would have snapped it in two or unspooled it, perhaps as Annalise had with one of his tapes, or at the very least told Ash she had thrown it away—anything to plunge the knife further into his regretful heart. The letter was cruel, but it could have, *should have* been crueller. It should have been brutal.

This was not written by Samantha, I didn't know who it was written by, but I would have bet all I had left in the world at that moment that the letter had been sent from Paris but by another's hands.

I have met my fair share of cruel people. Perhaps others think the same of me. I have said things I didn't mean when drunk; I have hit back to save face; but I have never held out my hand to greet someone I knew well and then, because of some imagined slight, asked them what their name was again. We are all capable of cruelty. Some is delivered under the banner of another psyche, the influence of the smoke-filled room and pain; the rest is handed out as if by a jester, a narcissist who sees it as their job to shape the world to their unholy vision—who thinks it's a game.

A game, a game, all a game... I left my office and found one of the young International Relations Unit officers who was packing up for the day, but I was always happy to help them out with an extra job. I asked them to find the files on a particular name and any source of handwriting we might have on file. They annoyed me by calling me by my rank. I preferred 'Detective'; titles made me think of my father, and how he would have gone further up the chain of command had it not been for my stupidity.

I smiled weakly and thanked them, not their fault. I deserved it, I guess. A small moment of cruelty will always bounce back at you. It wouldn't take long.

I returned to my office and attempted to make small talk with Rose, but suddenly the job had become too difficult. How to involve a dead man in your investigation—one who had been a shadow in your own life, a curse that had blighted your name.

We are chained to our past foes. We cannot outrun them as they move silently up the board, some being sacrificed, others making it all the way to the top, crowned king or queen of memories. Mine were self-induced, born of a desire to be something other than what my father and mother envisaged. Ash Corrish, even Rose, had been dragged into this world unsuspectingly, and all because of a chance encounter at a Cleveland bus station. But that is what life is: random connections, the unkind and the beautiful; it is also a form of future punishment. We cannot say all we want to for fear of upsetting perceived karma. A normal person will bite their tongue, but that swelling of the rough edge, that burning sensation—it is the moment in which you could have freed yourself and instead becomes a prison.

Fear makes prisoners of us all. I had not truly lived up to my position since I returned, content to ignore the problems rather than solve them. I had allowed, arguably encouraged my life to be one of procedure rather than finding the truth. I fooled myself that I had done my best, patted myself on the back for being in a position of respect again, yet I had done nothing to earn it. Could I have averted Corrish's beating? I did it all by the book; but I had also turned a blind eye to the possibility of there still being a corrupt element inside the police force. I hadn't gone after them, leaving, *trusting* all that to my superiors.

In silence, and with the pretence of reading through once more the stack of letters in front of me, I thought of Corrish. I thought of Captain Holt—why had he taken such a risk and told me a lie when I would have helped if he had asked me? I thought of Rose, sitting on the other side of my desk, her eyes closed as if in prayer, her lips asking for guidance from a god I had long since disowned. I thought of my friend, now dead, his ashes scattered to the winds, his home burned down and now a rubble-strewn site. I thought of the Spider, and the only connection I could think of that tied us all together was Catherine Ó Foghladh.

I turned on the computer and waited for several moments while it spluttered to life, the action causing Rose to open her eyes to see what was occurring and then close them once again, seemingly satisfied her prayers were having some effect.

Catherine Ó Foghladh, businesswoman, high-flyer, striking picture accompanying the page on the internet, an almost dead ringer for her sister. *Dig deeper.* Her father murdered, crime never solved, no mention of Samantha. *Strange.* Running for office in her home city of Cleveland, returned home after the 9/11 attacks on New York and Washington. Another picture, looking relaxed in front of a cabinet of books and a mountain of albums stacked neatly in alphabetical order. Studied French Art in Paris, no mention of kids, nor a husband. *Dig deeper still. The rumours we seek out to provide a clearer picture.*

There, finally, was a picture of her sister, quite young, a pleasant face but her eyes seemed haunted. A temper to match Catherine's, if the report were to be believed. Rumours but no proof that their father's murder was a hit, but the details didn't add up. The coroner expressed a concern that the cut to the top of his head didn't match the ferocity of the knives jammed into his eyes. That he was a handler for the IRA was known but kept on the down-low by officers at the time.

There was no placing of Catherine for several months while she was supposed to be in Paris, followed by a picture of her with him at a benefit dinner. She looked different, somehow, less self-assured compared to the picture which crowned her fame and pushed her into the limelight, as if she had been through a trauma. *The timeframe…* She was not in Paris when the letter was sent; the authorities had not been able to reach her to let her know that her father had died until some months after.

I returned to the picture of her relaxing, a pose for the photographer. I imagined him remarking on her collection and her blasé reply asking why a woman should not have eclectic tastes in art. I could read some of the spines—lots of jazz, some blues, French words I could not easily translate, tapes galore.

I was abruptly pulled out of this world without warning when the International Relations Unit officer knocked on the door sharply. I think it amused them to knock me off my stride, a small payback for keeping them back. They passed over the files and asked if that was all. I replied it was and in act of penance enquired as to their plans for the evening. I could not help but frown with dejection when I was informed that tonight there was a poetry festival in Valletta, my favourite Maltese Songbird being the top of the bill. I had forgotten.

I bade them have a great evening and told them to pass on my best should they speak to any of the poets. A small return of mercy, they told me they would, and then, just as they were leaving, they turned back and suggested that perhaps I should turn on my phone. The desk had some messages for me, including one from the chief, who sounded quite irritated that I had gone dark, as he had news that he must immediately get to me.

There were several other messages: one from Aakster's mother, asking me to call at my earliest convenience, one from Captain Holt, which didn't make much sense, and another from Catherine Ó Foghladh—could I Skype her as soon as possible? Trying not to be a jerk but also maintaining professional distance,

I thanked the International Relations Unit officer and told them I would deal with the calls directly.

When they'd left, I turned my attention to the boxes they had brought me. What I was after should have been quite near the top of the pile, and as I shuffled through the Spider's complex web, I came across the first of the results I was looking for. I passed the sheet of paper across to Rose and asked her to examine it alongside the writing that had made up the letter from Paris. While she did that, I fished through the rest of the files until I found the page of known addresses that would confirm my suspicions.

Rose looked up from studying the two sets of handwriting. Like me, she was no expert on the subject, but she confirmed there was more of a suggestion that both the letter and the other sample were written by the same person. She was confused, and I didn't blame her. Nothing about this was straightforward, but life isn't meant to be.

Chapter Eighteen

We Are Bound Together, You and I

Catherine Ó Foghladh

I CAN FEEL IT all slipping out of my control, everything I have fought for draining away. From the moment I was old enough to realise what a shit storm I had been born into, I have tried to rise above it. Even getting pregnant at sixteen didn't deter me from proving I was better than the life my father had marked out for me.

But every wrong turn has been beset by trusting the wrong man. It was bad enough trusting Marshall. I paid for that mistake for nearly a year, sweating it out in New York, waiting to go back to my Paris home, living with a man who made me call him husband, who trapped me as much as my father had.

I trusted Holt to get the job done. He owed me. He is the whole reason I am now having to save face and my political career by speaking to this Maltese detective.

We are bound together, all of us—you and me, dearest Samantha, you and Marshall—even in your death, I still have the connections I stole from you. I wept for you when I heard, but then I remembered everything you put me through, and my tears flowed only because the memory was so bitter. Still, without you, I would not be here now, on the cusp of something extraordinary, even if it has meant breaking several laws to achieve it.

It is my tie to you, Holt, that is the biggest. I wish I could sever it completely, take a sword to the rope that binds, pour gasoline over it, light a match and watch it burn. I think that might already be the case, but it is you who has held the match in the last few hours. Why couldn't you accept the chain of command and be the man I always thought you were?

Our web is stretched fine. I have never known a man, anyone, for as long as I have known you, and you don't even remember how we first met. I do, though, and if this goes wrong, you will say goodbye to your pension and that wife of yours. Always concerned with being regarded as a good cop, incorruptible, moral, made of the very character you ask the city to be seen in now…

You were a young rookie when you first tried to arrest my father on possession charges, an arrest quickly scrubbed from the records because you didn't know how the game worked. You were lucky you weren't taken into a back alley and given a beating for your disrespect. Only a quiet word in my father's ear saved you from that; you never did find that out, did you? Did you hear the rumours, the whispers that you were a dead man walking the streets of Cleveland for a while? I bet you didn't, you were so naïve.

But who am I to cast aspersions on naivety? I was never going to get help to return to Paris after Marshall caught me. Being held captive in New York for a year, lying low, no money to even escape with—the only time I left the rat-infested city was to attend a beach party where the man to which I was bound was also in attendance, supplying the drugs. Even then, I was accosted, pawed at by a *pissed-up Brit*, and it was in that meeting I found the one who could take the fall for it all.

My faith in you, Holt, has been stretched to the limit with the news you have been in contact with a colleague north of the border to investigate someone else for my father's murder. We all know it was Corrish, it had to be—the stranger who just happened to be in the city at the time. I have proved his whereabouts to you, but now I hear you don't trust me, think I've been leading you by the nose and have done this to give you a final hurrah, a final bow. Well, a bow to the audience as you retire is one thing; the press getting hold of our link is quite another. I do hope your heart can withstand the pressure.

I know you remember the night you found that young, frightened girl locked in the manager's office of one of the old games arcades that used to be part of many youths' lives, and while most were legitimate, some were used as fronts for moving anything illegal, all under the cover of a yellow maniac that killed ghosts and popped pills to the sound of repetitive, senseless music. I was young and so desperate to get out of town I had tried breaking into the office, knowing they took a lot of money on the weekend. I figured I could get in through the small back window, take the cash and leave as quickly as I had arrived. A business like that doesn't have great security, let alone a safe; the money was always just there, ready and bagged up. Everybody knew it, they just didn't dare try to bust the place because it was under the protection of one of meanest men in the area—my father.

You were the officer attending—why was that? Normally, it would have been someone who could be trusted to be discreet and make the person stupid enough to cross Beardsley suffer and disappear. I was glad it was you, though. By a twist of fate, my father never got to hear about it—I remember you telling me that the captain had bawled you out for letting me go, that you told him it had been a kid's dare and no harm was done. I was sixteen. I never gave you my real name, and it wasn't the first time I had given a man a blow job for his troubles. You insisted it wasn't necessary, but I could be very persuasive.

Sixteen. Such a sweet time in any girl's life, and there you were, to me, at that moment, a knight in Kevlar armour.

I hated the world, but in my teenage head, I loved you. For several months, you were my world. I often thought of getting in trouble again just so I could see you in the same light as the moment we first met, but then I might have had to tell you who I really was. It was easier to give you a false identity, to use a fake address, one of my few friends backing me up if you called. For you, I changed, at least outwardly; on the inside, I was full of rage. I didn't deserve to be fondled by my father's friends, to have their oversize sweaty man paws groping me, stroking my thighs, dribbling their versions of love into my ears, always with the pretence of *happy to please you* etched on my face.

My upbringing was one of disgust, but I feared for my sister. At that point, my father had not introduced her to any of the men who came calling—the dealers, the pimps, the foul and the offensive—but I knew in time, given the right persuasion, he would find a way to satisfy the needs of anybody willing to pay, in both cash and in future dealings.

There has always been you, though you broke it off quickly when you met the woman who would become your wife a few months later, and the secrets, such as they were, stopped being relevant. Gone was the wig; what need did I have of covering my hair with something so synthetic, so bogus, when my life was already that? I would see you on the street, and you would not recognise me at all, not now with a baby in my stomach, another life to care for.

That baby was both a curse and a blessing, and when my father punched me and I miscarried, I knew the curse was broken. I could finally plan my escape, no matter how long it took me to put it into execution.

Such naivety, such simple thought—get out of town and all will be well. It didn't work, not really—if it had, I would not be in this mess. I would be a curator in a French art gallery, for that is really what I wanted—to consume the only passion I had that didn't want to destroy me. When I left for France, when I managed to attain the necessary college scores that meant I could leave America, I put my father behind me and dreamed of sitting someday with a piece on my easel and people gathered behind me, occasionally selling one if only to have a conversation starter with friends and lovers.

Must look reasonable for this Maltese detective, make sure I appeal to his better nature. Do I have my story straight? Know the right questions to ask? *Don't forget to enquire about Mr. Corrish's present health, look concerned...* Concerned, just like Marshall was concerned for me while I was trapped in New York.

The plan had been simple: I would go to New York and meet Samantha, but then things went wrong. I arrived and saw her waiting, a young man by her side, holding her hand, worry on his face. She looked unwell. I had thought about the moment of reconnection for so long, I just wanted to sweep her up, to hold my baby sister again and make amends for having left in the first place. She always told me that she understood, but I knew I had been selfish. I had protested that I loved her, that I was concerned for her well-being, but if it were true, I would have stayed or fought my father and taken her with me.

Such fine words for a woman running for office. It makes a mockery of my lies, the backtracking and investigations I have had to endure, and not one of those has told me who killed my father. I mean, don't get me wrong: I hated him. But the way he died, well, any but the stoniest of hearts would hunt down the perpetrators and seek vengeance.

I didn't learn of his death for almost a year, not until I returned to Paris. Marshall knew and didn't tell me even though I spoke to him quite often. I was trapped in New York; I had nowhere to go, and despite being told initially it was just for a couple of days, Marshall had changed his mind, or rather, he suggested it was too difficult to get me home again, I would have to wait, bide my time.

While he never outwardly admitted it, I knew he was punishing me. *Don't worry yourself. I will take care of the apartment. I will look after your arrangements, don't concern yourself with anything,*

just stay in the shadows for a while. You are a wanted woman...
too dangerous to come back now.

In the year I was there, I never came across any news item indicating I was a suspect...such bullshit. But without a passport, without any money, I had no choice but to believe him and hope for the best.

It was fun to throw a wrench into the works of Marshall's cleverly orchestrated plan, the unseen fly scraping its feet over the slow-grilled steak. I suspect that was why he punished me, cutting me off from the life that I had made in Paris.

If ever I felt victorious, it would have been at that moment. I had to tell him she had promised to write to someone when she arrived in Paris. I had asked who, and that memory remained. Now, looking back, I am pretty certain I didn't have to do that. The man unconscious in a Maltese hospital would never have bothered with her; it is only because he became so lonely he decided to reconnect with his past.

It would be easy to dismiss the man as a fool—most men are— but his actions of nostalgia set all this in motion, and if I have to see it through, if I have to bring down a captain, a man I have never met and that fool at the same time, then by heavens, I will.

I have a few minutes before the Maltese detective calls me. I shall play this calmly but with authority. After all, I'm running for office. I could piss all over his life from there—he forgets I am somebody.

***

I have no idea what just happened. We were talking via Skype, I was answering his questions, and all was going well. After about twenty minutes, I saw his eyes begin to wander, not away from the screen but as if he was searching the background, looking at what was behind me instead of directly at my face. We continued talking for a while, but I was irritated by his lack of respect, and I completely missed a question and had to ask him to repeat it.

Yes, of course I lived in Paris, it is a matter of public knowledge. If that initial question threw me, then what followed completely unnerved me. Yes, I lived at that address. No, I did not know Marshall Rhagodidae. Sorry, you must be mistaken, his name was never on the building's tenancy agreement. Do I know a man by the name of Capone? No. Did I pay Capone to assault Mr. Corrish? No!

Then my interrogator's eyes seemed to settle on something just over my left shoulder, only for a second, but it was enough for me to want to terminate the interview, although what could he do all the way over there on that tiny, forgettable island?

He beat me to it, though. He was polite and gracious, but something about his demeanour had changed. He tried to brush it off as having had a message come through from his superiors to say he was needed elsewhere. There was no *I'll call back later*, just a "Thank you for everything, the conversation has been illuminating."

I turned off Skype and sat back in my chair. I was contemplating making a call when the phone rang. Half expecting it to be the detective, I answered with a sneer. It was one of the city's lawyers informing me that a man I had gotten to know through my association with Marshall had been arrested. He only had the one phone call, but he'd had the sense to not call me directly. He'd been arrested in connection with the attack on Corrish.

No sooner had I put the phone down than I received another call, this time from Holt. He was being driven to my office. "Is that wise in your condition?" I asked. He grumpily replied that he had no choice, he had to see me face-to-face. It would not be official, he was not in uniform, but it was urgent.

For the first time since I was ostracised in New York, since having to share a bed with a man who treated me like shit and made sure I was in no fit state to leave, I felt the walls of my castle being stormed and broken down. It was all coming undone. I knew the moment had passed, I should have just left it alone.

The strong-woman act had become paper-thin, but I was not going to lie down and take it. This was the second time I would have a gun in my hand, and as with my dear captor, I would be happy to use it when the time presented itself.

Ah, Marshall, you taught me well. You exiled me across the ocean, and I put a bullet in your friend's head. It wasn't the first time I had killed. My sister, wherever she is, could attest to that. So come at me, Captain Holt. Come with your news. Question me if you must, but you forget one thing. I know something you have kept under that moral hat of yours. You slept with me. Admittedly, I told you I was older than I was, but that won't save you. I might not put a gun against your head, but I will blow your life away should you do anything rash.

Chapter Nineteen

We Did It for the Money and the Kicks

A Native American Admits to Murder

M Y FRIEND IS dead, and I don't have long to live, so this will come as a relief, plus you will not be able to put me in prison. I have served my time with the disease in my veins, and now I wish to sit at the fires of my ancestors with a clean spirit.

I will tell you, though, that you are doing the dirty work of the white man. Now there is your disease, one that has forever tainted our lands and taken from us all that belonged to our brothers and sisters, to our children and grandchildren yet to come. If that makes this all right for you then let it be so. I will do my best to explain, and yes, for the record, I shall do so in that frightening English tongue. Does it save you from translating for all those involved? Fine, Luqi.

The events are from my point of view. My friend will not be able to defend himself or his honour. His tainted soul now rests, and while you can drag his name through the investigation, he will ride and hunt buffalo with the rest of the First Nation tribe for eternity. For what he did was just. You might not think so, lawman, but tell me, do you feel special being involved with the police of America, a country divided by its struggle against itself? I read the news: the president is an imnakuluk, and the world is heading for extinction, but yes, you can question me all you want about something that took place three decades ago.

Why do you work for the white man? No, forget that, it is obvious. You were the product of a union between the two tribes, your mother was one of us? I feel contempt for you, although it hasn't always been this way. I knew a man once, honourable, perhaps the only white man I have met that was. He came to us with his hand outstretched and willing to learn, and from the short time he was in our company, we looked to him as one of our own. He may not have been pure blood, but he acted as if he was, and it was a sad day when my friend and I were instructed to get him back across the American border so he could avoid being caught as an illegal.

The chain of events is such that had we not been helping Ashkii, then we might not have gone to Cleveland, and from there, we would not have killed that man, although in truth I took great delight in being part of that moment. Another piece of white trash off the streets, one who brought misery to the community. We know how to deal with such problems. What do you do? You send them to jail, believing you can reform them, but they become a scourge, a disease, which takes others down with them.

He would have had his revenge, though, our own fault, and my friend was ostracised because of his greed. I see every day the problems with disease and how you prolong it for your economy, the people of Western Africa that have seen their communities destroyed by Ebola because they cannot begin to fight a disease that the Western governments introduced into society to keep the numbers down. It was the same with AIDS—it only became a concern when straight white people started dying, when entertainers suddenly became infected. You are all the same, and you—you compound it by doing their bidding. Was it a white police chief that sent you after me?

My friend, he died of AIDS. He contracted it through a shared needle. A shipment of drugs found its way to our settlement. I don't know who sent it, but I can guess. Cheap and mixed, the poison he put into his veins, that turned him into an addict, that saw him seek out cheap alternatives in Detroit and Buffalo. But it was when we were doing a job in New York that he made his pact with the dead, a shared needle in some back-street kitchen in Harlem.

I never saw the point of it, always avoiding the shit and trying my hardest to keep my friend away from it. He was a free spirit, an artist—it was his idea to put the knives in the man's eyes, a logical step up from our ancestors who would scalp their intended victim. I went along with that; we were in it for the kicks and the money.

There were so many clues that my friend wasn't well, but we didn't have the education to see it for what it was. He lost weight, and I put it down to him being an addict. By 1992, millions were infected, many of whom died, but it was unknown in our corner of the world. We had no guide; our elders refused to let outsiders come into our lives again after Ashkii left, not wanting to be found in their company. I blame them as much as I blame you for the aftermath of that.

My friend didn't last long, that was a mercy. But it was the ignominy which became a source of disgust for me. Moved to one of the islands that could be seen from the shore, he was treated as if he had the plague. He was given food but told not to have any contact with the tribe, including his mother, from the day the lesions started appearing on his body. The tribe prayed for guidance; natural medicines were made then eventually discarded as he became progressively worse.

He died, whether from withdrawal, from the disease or from being uncared for, I do not know, but the disease was just a part of the end of his life.

You ask me why I killed that man in Cleveland. Because he was part of this chain. He was a link to the point when I believe the problems between my people and those who seek to destroy our way of life overlap.

I do not blame the tribe, or my family, for the way they dealt with my friend's death. They were ignorant of the facts, but that doesn't change the way I feel about you. I have little time in front of me and no regard for the future, but I want, *need*, to put down my words of contempt.

It seems the addiction to the white powder and sexual disease has crossed boundaries as easily as musical taste and gambling. Throw in the nastiness, soul-breaking sorrow and the blackening of cancer and you have a potent mix of humanity having lost control.

I was diagnosed six months ago. Aggressive and quick, they promised me, and my tribe has been supportive this time. They have treated me as if I am on my way to the old hunting grounds. Everything I want in life has become mine, such a far cry from the way my friend was treated. I don't know if you call it cultural, or if, somehow, they are making amends. In the end, it doesn't really matter to me; I shall soon blow into the night and let my spirit wander.

You see, even when I tell you the name of the man who hired us to kill that Irish joker, that dealer of men, I will walk out of here a free man. I came here voluntarily, I am not under arrest, and I am only talking to you now to pay a small debt to Ashkii. My time is up, but I hope Ashkii's is long and fruitful.

Ashkii first came to the area as a soul devoid of hope. He had questions but few demands. If he had not stayed that one night and talked, I guess he would have gone on forever, from one township to the next, always being guided by the sound of his heart. He was troubled, a double spirit, a dominant timber wolf and a mewling cub fighting over the scraps of life and knowledge to feed and nurture their sinew and their pulse. He was sick, not in the way that you and I get sick. He had no terrible disease ravaging his body, he had no addiction, save that which he had buried deep in his soul. His sickness was one he wanted to cleanse, he required healing, and for a short time, we were able to assist. We chose to help this outsider and for no other reason than the way he presented humility in front of us.

This was not a man who came into our lives with bluster and threats, a white heart; this was a man willing to learn and, in some ways, to teach. He certainly taught me a few things, least of all acceptance in my own troubled soul.

Over there on the shoreline, where that exposed large rock juts out pointing to the north, I felt accepted without having been made to feel dirty, and while he would not feel the same way, he smiled and told me it didn't matter, that even my father, a man of proud traditions and no nonsense, would in time be all right with my decision, as long as I was honest.

I championed his cause; I drove him away.

You may have turned your soul away from the old ways, you have embraced the ways of the white man and the sick, but sometimes someone will come into your life who defies your expectations. For me, that was Ashkii. I cannot talk for my friend, not because I didn't know what he thought, but he is long since in the company of our ancestors and I will not defile his wandering soul with gossip. All you need to know is that he was there with me when we drove down through Ontario, stopping off in Niagara to make sure we would be safe getting across, always choosing the right moment and reason to dare to try such a thing, down through Buffalo and on to Cleveland.

It seemed the best approach in the end. I was all for taking Ashkii across country as far as Vancouver, even taking the road down to Kitchener and on to Detroit, but Ashkii realised he might never be able to come back this way, and for his own peace of mind he wanted to see the old lumber and steel towns of Hamilton and Niagara Falls one last time. Who am I to tell a brother what he can and cannot do? Those are your rules, right?

We drove, my friend and I taking turns at the wheel, but always with Ashkii in the front passenger seat. We wanted him to see the forests, to take in what he was leaving behind and savour the open road. I heard him utter once the word *majestic* when we spotted some of the local wildlife crossing in front of us. He was that sort of man: white heart, native soul.

We dropped him off in Hamilton for the night and we drove on a little further, not wanting to get mixed up with the locals. He got out of the car and walked purposefully to a bar called The Gown and Gavel. He told us the next morning that he stayed there for a few hours, just talking, playing pool, remembering what it was like to once more be part of a ritual. He wasn't sure when he would ever be able to do something as mundane again. I didn't blame him for it. I think he had earned that right. Besides, he had paid us for the gas and for our time.

I think it was a rite of passage for him. He had come to find out about his grandfather, and in an era of suspicion, he broke down a wall I had forcibly erected. That entire day he spent wandering around the town, he'd ended up in a congregation at one of the local churches, not because he was religious, but because he wanted to observe the difference in cultures after spending so much time with us. He probably doesn't know, but that church on King Street has been knocked down now, flattened, destroyed, erased of its memory—so much for those early Baptists proclaiming that the word of God lasts forever.

I have been to Hamilton recently, a fine place for a Western heart. I wanted to take a look at what had intrigued Ashkii. I am not sure he would care for it; whatever it was that captivated him about the town has been spirited away. The Gown and Gavel is still there, but it no longer has a pool table, and the church has gone. The sense of the small community has been replaced by big commerce. Toronto has spread its tentacles outwards—that is your undoing. Always, you encroach. You intrude on what is beyond life, you seek to violate yet call it influence. You have no peace with the world; it is no wonder it is rebelling against you.

The next morning, we drove to Niagara Falls, and it was there I saw Ashkii openly weep from a distance as he stared at that waterfall for over an hour. I never found out what was going on in his head. I never asked. To me, it seemed a private, deeply spiritual moment in which the two spirits were merging into one. He had found peace, briefly, transiently. We waited in the car, not wishing to draw attention to ourselves, and it was there that I took a phone call from an old friend of mine who used to smuggle alcohol across the border. Do you remember those old phones—awkward but somehow required? He asked me if I would be up for a job; I replied I was. It wasn't until we had left Ashkii at the station in Cleveland that the job became apparent.

I would like to believe that had we not driven Ashkii across the border, had we not realised that someone was looking for him, had he not entered our lives, my friend and I would not have ended up at that address that day and killed the Irishman. The consequence of our actions is that we can look back at the exact moment when we believe our lives took a different path and understand it was always going to be, regardless.

You ask me do I regret taking on the contract to kill the Irishman. Not at all, and that is the truth. I have nothing to lose. In a moment, I am going to stand up, shake your hand and leave. You will not chase me; you will honour that I will meet my ancestors, my father and my dear love in my own way, not in bondage, not tied to your laws. You have all the proof you need. Your tape is still running. I will sign my name, but you will not stop me from pursuing my own path.

Ashkii went inside the Greyhound bus station without saying goodbye. There was a smile on his face when he looked back the once, but there was nothing to say.

I don't think he was concentrating, his mind full once more of the trials of his heart. It is easy to be consumed by your world. It only takes a certain action to absorb any person into the blackness. I watched as he walked through the door to the station—he never even noticed the pretty young girl just a step or two behind him, her bag weighed down with her guilt, her soul heavy with the journey ahead. It was the last time I saw Ashkii. I wish I had gotten to know him better. I wish we hadn't taken him to Cleveland. My friend might still be alive, for I believe had we not killed that man, had we not taken a job from Marshall Rhagodidae, then his life would have been different. He would not have been tortured by disgust for what he did. He would not have gone on to destroy his soul, the spirit of his fathers and mothers before him.

All it took was a needle that had been infected with a disease you could have stopped. He died because he could not bear what he had become—my own salvation has been long in the reckoning. Thank you, Officer, for allowing me this chance to put a record straight. If you speak to anyone who knows Ashkii, please tell them to pass on a message: tell Ashkii I thank him. He was a good man. He didn't judge, he gave me strength in my own fight, and he had a noble soul.

Now...now is my time to depart. I don't have long; the timber wolves are prowling, circling the camp, their fierce growls haunting me, and they have begun to gnaw and tear at my open stomach. It is time to let them feast.

Chapter Twenty

Kept in the Dark

The Detective

I PAUSED THE IMAGE again and stared hard beyond Ms. Ó Foghladh's head. No matter how much I strained my eyes or tried to enhance the picture, what I wanted to focus on was still just a blur, a view of possible misconception. In my heart, I knew I had seen something that didn't fit in her story, yet fitted perfectly in with Ashkii Corrish's.

Rose was sitting with the now-awake Ash, a touching reunion of friends to which we should not have been witness, and yet they seemed grateful for the company. Ash had woken suddenly, almost as if a thousand volts had been pushed through him. Such was the jerk of alertness that came from the bed that the chief, who had been sitting beside him, lost in the steam of a freshly brewed coffee, dropped the ceramic mug onto the floor as the roar of life filled the room.

When we arrived at the hospital, the chief was taking notes, the urgency of the moment suspended as Ashkii Corrish spotted his friend and leaned forward to embrace her. In another world, I suspected they may have been lovers; they were too close to just be friends, but then it is a world that is alien to me, not really ever having any friends who were platonic. The closest I guess I had was with my Magpie, and even then I sometimes had to take a different tack with her. She had been part of my thoughts for such a long time, but it would not be right in the circumstances.

I motioned to the chief that we should give them some space and told them we would be back in half an hour. I gave Melina Borg instructions to secure the point of entry to the room.

We walked out into the grounds of the hospital, and the chief offered me a cigarette, filthy habit. I accepted and waited for him to light the tip before telling him what I had found out after comparing the writing on the letter to Corrish and some of the documented writing of Marshall Rhagodidae. The chief didn't say a word. He frowned in concentration and took a long drag of his cigarette, carefully blowing the smoke out of his nose, resembling a pondering dragon unsure whether it wanted to destroy the village or eat the knight who had sworn his life and honour to the princess in the ivory tower.

I then told him about the conversation with Ms. Ó Foghladh and showed him the image I had recorded. At that, he smiled. "A cassette tape," he remarked, but like me, he could not initially understand why a single cassette tape would be on show surrounded by expensive-looking legal books.

A single tape, just waiting to be heard.

I finished my cigarette and pressed it out against a coin that I had taken out of my pocket before I put it in the tray on top of the bin a few feet away. Coming back to my superior's side, I spoke softly; I didn't want any of the staff or other patients to overhear words that could be taken out of context.

I told him I had checked on the apartment that Ms. Ó Foghladh had been living for most of her time in Paris. It was owned by the man I had killed eighteen months before. There was no shadow of doubt that she had lied to me. On that alone, I had called the captain in Cleveland and told him my concerns, who Marshall Rhagodidae was, and while the captain was clearly unwell, he was able to impart to me that he had heard from a detective friend in Canada who had interviewed one of the names I had given him from Corrish's interview. He had not arrested him; there was little point. The man was dying of cancer and wouldn't speak on the record, but he too had confirmed the name of the man who almost took my life.

I tried calling the captain again, but it took an age to go through and instead clicked over to voicemail. With the chief closely listening, I asked Captain Holt if he would send a couple of men over to Ms. Ó Foghladh's office and arrest her, use anything he could to see her removed from the premises.

Anybody who had consorted with Rhagodidae was not to be trusted—the irony was not lost on me that such a notion should have included me.

As I made my farewells to Holt's voicemail, the chief took a call from headquarters: one of the police sergeants had arrested the young constable who had been in the interview room on suspicion of having aided Capone in his entry into the holding area. He had managed to turn off the recording equipment inside and by the gate but had forgotten about the camera on the main street, where he was seen talking to Capone fifteen minutes prior to the assault. Again, all these links were not yet proven, but it was telling that the officer had called his lawyer, and who had his lawyer called? Ms. Foghladh! Curiously, it seemed the lawyer had called the assistant commissioner to inform him of this act. When asked why, he said he could not have it on his conscience, even if he was on a retainer with the woman.

The chief told the sergeant that he understood, and was informed of a couple of other pieces of news. An actress who had been working in Malta had been found dead on the stage, and a planned protest outside the Courts of Justice building that evening was concerning the deputy commissioner. I asked if it was anything I could attend to, but the chief shook his head, telling me I had enough on my plate.

Noticing that a half hour had gone past, we started to make our way back inside the hospital. At the entrance, my phone rang. Expecting it to be Captain Holt telling me he had received my message, I told the chief I would catch up with him. He nodded politely and walked on, leaving me to turn back a few steps to avoid being in the way of the hospital doors and the revolving thoughts of visitors laden with flowers.

I looked down at the screen; it wasn't Holt. It was Aakster's mother. I answered it without hesitation.

There are times when your life crumbles, others when it is brutally torn apart. You will recognise them by the way someone greets you—that important interview upon which you have hung all your hopes for the future, dashed in the moment they tell you *this won't take long*. Or in that handshake weakly offered, ostensibly a sign of friendship but in fact the act of the social terrorist committing the modern-day equivalent of Judas kissing the cheek of his supposed pal. Or the offer of a drink and a sit-down as they show you their concerned face. It is these moments that crumble your faith.

The ones that tear your life apart are those that come out of nowhere. I forget exactly how I reacted when my ex-wife told me she wanted a divorce. Too much time has gone under the bridge, but I know I was sick to my stomach, the same intense feeling washing over me as the day when my father found out I had fallen in the pathway of a devil, and when my sister was pronounced dead at the beach. I had the same feeling hit me even before I heard Aakster's mother say my name. Desperation hung in the air, like the sirens that sounded before the planes were heard and my grandparents took shelter in the caves under Valletta, or the people of Liverpool and London, of Hamburg and Dresden in the final throes of World War Two. I placed my ear against the phone and told her I was here.

Her voice was low, distant, apologetic, almost as if I were a priest listening to confession from a previous unblemished soul. The words all came out in a garbled mess, unsure of which sin to profess first and how the person behind the latticed frame would react, the curtain slightly open so the congregation could witness the fall of the once just, the priest safe from the prying eyes of the mob waiting to add something to their gossip, all bluster.

In this open-air confessional, the local birds acted as a youthful choir joining in the hymn, or as a Greek Chorus ready to expose their hearts to the Mediterranean heavens as Troy falls. The memory of Aakster, my friend, became one shrouded in mystery and sorrow. In this unlikely confessional, I heard her mother apologise to me, seek forgiveness when I could see no reason to have even thought to blame. When you are vulnerable, you carry the burden of the world upon your shoulders. You are susceptible to attack, and most of it is of your imagination. I don't have a problem with a lie; it is how it formed that is important. If it comes from a good place, to spare someone worry, to show them compassion, and not created to kick someone when they are down and almost out, then no confession is required, especially when the news was as profound as this was.

I let her speak, tell me the details, and I didn't interrupt. I made no noise, no admission of concern until she was ready to stop. I didn't know her that well—she must have thought I was a wreck the last time she met me, sitting in a bar in Haarlem not far from their family home, the early morning vodka shots doing their best to numb the pain and lighten my mood. If she thought I was out of my mind, she didn't show it as she took my hand gently, tenderly putting the glass out of my reach and asking me to tell her about my relationship with a servant of evil.

We stayed in that bar for two hours, talking about Aakster's aunt, who had been part of the story, the welcome they gave Rhagodidae into their home as he slowly destroyed her will. We were connected, and she didn't judge my part in the life of the man who would die in the tunnels of Valletta. She just listened; it was a relief to show her the same compassion and courtesy as she unburdened her soul.

I asked if there was anything I could do to help, the news hitting me hard, but still, I was able to make the sincere gesture of a friend—that if she needed me then I would come as soon as this case was solved. She thanked me and sought forgiveness for keeping me in the dark. I understood. She hadn't wanted me to worry. I would leave the confessional box at the same time as her. I would show the awaiting hyenas in the pews that some sins are not worth examining. I would take her by the hand and kiss her kindly on the cheek and ask the congregation to do the same.

We said our goodbyes, she promised to call if any further news came her way. I promised to do the same, and then all was quiet. The chorus and the hymnals became silent. In one of the busiest places on the island, I felt alone. Aakster, my dear Magpie. How will your mother cope?

I wanted to cry, to walk away from this place of pity and sadness. I wanted to go home, change out of these damn repressive clothes and head to the airport and catch a flight to Holland, but there was nothing I could do for now; Aakster wasn't going anywhere. I just had to wait by the phone. Thankfully, the job, I was sure, was almost over.

I walked through the corridors, the world emerging once more, the rush of nurses, doctors studying clipboards, equipment being moved, the odd sounds of laughter, the cries of a child as its leg was reset and placed in a cast—this was the real tragedy and the hospital was the chorus.

Eventually, I returned to Corrish's room and asked Melina Borg if she wouldn't mind getting me a cup of tea. Normally, I would not have asked such a question, but she must have noticed my agitated state as she readily agreed. I knocked on the door and walked in, not waiting for the confirmation from my chief or Corrish or Rose.

The chief scrutinised me, contemplating the deep furrow and lines that must surely have appeared in the last twenty minutes. He asked if the call had been Holt. I didn't reply. I made a gesture that I would talk to him afterwards; he seemed to understand and let it go. Instead, he spoke of what Corrish had told him, adding to his statement a night in New Jersey, a party on the beach where he thought he had seen Samantha but it turned out to be a woman called Abigael Wells, how he had wandered out to the sea and thrown his Walkman at the approaching police boat and cracked the screen. It may have been a dream, but he knew it was a memory resurfacing.

Corrish had been given a pill, something he would normally have shied away from, but the evening had taken on a weird vibe. Lots of dope, the resulting trauma of being arrested and sent back to England and the subsequent hospitalisation a couple of years later had drowned so many memories. Throughout, I watched Rose watching him. I guessed she was wondering if any other memories might resurface, whether his sister Annalise was in for a rude awakening when he returned. He wouldn't be able to continue living on the island; the university would not like the adverse publicity. I suspected they would not seek to employ another British lecturer for a while.

I felt angry, resentment boiling away in my stomach—not at Corrish. Like so many, he was just another soul reaching out for someone to grab his hand. I didn't help matters by asking if he knew that one of the men who'd helped him across the Canadian border had died. Fury flashed across my chief's face. He kept quiet, but I saw his hand curl up tightly into a ball.

There was a knock at the door. I opened it and Melina Borg handed me the cup of tea. I no longer wanted it and passed it to Corrish, apologising for my lack of tact. He smiled and told me it was not a problem. It had been a long time since those days, and he needed to move on. Then, just as I was about to leave, he remembered something else.

"The tape. It was in the man's pocket."

He explained that it was *his* tape, which he had given to Samantha. He didn't really buy anything other than vinyl, and he couldn't carry those when he travelled, so he made tapes and drew pictures on the labels, making his own front covers.

He'd given a Nirvana tape to Samantha as he left the bus, and it was in the man's pocket—the man who was with Abigael Wells that night.

I watched the chief make a note of the name and where Corrish said she had come from. The chief asked Borg to remain with Corrish and Rose, and he and I left the room and walked out of the building. He rounded on me as soon as we were outside—a dressing-down on tact—and I held up my hands to acknowledge my mistake. Not that my defence was sound, but I explained who the phone call had been from, that Aakster's father had suffered a stroke a few days ago and had died as a result. The chief softened and asked if Aakster was all right; he knew she was close to her parents. I opened my mouth to reply, but it took a minute to get the words out. I was aware I was breaking the seal of the confessional, violating the trust of the congregation.

I could barely bring myself to tell him, so, like Aakster's mother, I blurted it out. Aakster had gone missing. She wasn't aware her father was dead. It seemed she was investigating a case in England and last checked in with her parents eight days ago, then suddenly, according to her superior, she just went off the grid. She had disappeared.

Chapter Twenty-One

Part of a Missing Girl's Journal, 1992

In New York City

It seems apt that the first album the man played for me as I sat in his flat above the bar he owned, was *The Lamb Lies Down on Broadway*. I was not of that era. I had no personal connection with the times the lyrics spoke of, yet it resonated with me. A girl in the shadow of the anti-hero, Rael, the half Puerto Rican petty graffiti artist who comments on the consumerism and the sexual revolution of the time. There was more to this boy, though, this split personality, and I identified with him as I pored over the lyrics and let the music wash over me like spray paint on a bland wall. I was soon covered with imagery and the distaste of life; I have come so far in such a short time, but there was still a long way to go.

I saw faces and traces of home…back in Cleveland, on the road. I have seen the best and worst of people, and I have been the cause of that suffering. Now I am just a short step away from escaping.

I telephoned my sister as soon as I made it to New York. I could not tell initially if she was angry with me. I still had some money but not enough to make the flight that she had arranged, and the passport was gone. She told me she would fix it for me and to meet her in two days' time at the airport. I still needed help; I had nowhere to clean the dust of the last few days from my skin, I was exhausted; I need to lay my head down and think, so I did the only thing I could. I took a chance on the man whose number I had been given by the Amish woman on the Greyhound bus, and with a heart that felt as if it was going to burst from beating, I dialled and waited for an answer.

I placed my trust in an Englishman in New York.

When he answered, I blurted out who I was and who had told me to contact him if I was in trouble. He asked if I was Amish, and I felt as if he was going to put the phone down on me when I admitted that I wasn't. The line stayed silent for a few seconds before he spoke again and asked where I was. I told him I was at Penn Station, looking up at the architecture on the ceiling. That made him laugh. He agreed to help and would meet me on the corner of 79th Street—just get the uptown subway, what was I wearing. He would not be long, not to worry.

Even after all the voyages of the last few days, I was nervous. I read a book once that explained the problems with being on the run. You are forever looking over your shoulder, never quite sure who is a friend and who is out to bleed you dry. Several times in the last few days I have had the urge to go back home, to seek forgiveness from my father. I know I left him unconscious in our home, but he would be all right—a little battered, a little sore— then I remember all that he will do to me in return. Scars heal, but the memory of them being inflicted always remains.

Running is what I have become good at, hiding in the shadows, and it was with that armour surrounding me that I made my way to 79th Street. The underground was like nothing I had ever experienced before; all manner of life was there, and despite assurances that it wasn't as bad as it used to be, there was still an unnerving sense of fear that ran through my body. The darkness outside the windows was pitch-black streaked with the flashes of light you might expect from seeing an electrical storm over the Great Lakes—blinding, painful—and yet there was a sense of life there, unnatural, as if the tunnel harboured nocturnal creatures that would spit at your face if you got too close to seeing their true image. Row upon row, a microsecond elapsing before the next shot past, the glass saving the venom from reaching me, these electrical bats hanging forever in the darkness, extraordinary creatures born from the cheerless world underneath the great metropolis.

I stumbled out of the subway as if I had returned from the outer fringes of a great war, tired, seeing images that weren't there. I had ignored the claims of a man insisting he was Jesus, proclaiming death to all non-believers but who also had a ham on rye sandwich in his left hand slowly dripping mayo onto the subway car's floor. I kept my eyes averted from the young black man in the suit making notes with a pencil. I turned away from the Hispanic woman who constantly swore and then laughed, causing those near her to either gasp in fright at the unholy scene or to secretly smile, invisibly egging her on, enjoying the depth of character one must possess to live in the Big Apple and root through its core.

The sun blinded me, but in that exchange of dark and light, I felt the stirrings of rebirth. Against the odds, I had made it this far. I was sucked back into the dark as a shadow descended on me, and I almost screamed as a hand clutched my shoulder and a voice asked me for my name. I punched out and thankfully didn't connect with the person who had scared the life out of me. For his part, he immediately apologised.

He introduced himself as Jack Colquhoun, a runaway as well—"But," he added softly, "my story is nowhere near as exciting as yours, I bet." I smiled and liked him immediately. He asked if I wanted a coffee and something to eat. He wanted to ask me more questions before taking me to his place. When you are on the run, you don't know who to trust, and sometimes you make bad decisions. Sometimes you get pulled in. They tell you that you are beautiful, that you're the only woman who makes them feel special, and before you know it, you're in trouble, part of a system which is designed to keep you subdued, a prisoner, a dead woman no one remembers; not every stranger is a friend in the making, some are just that: strange.

There was something about Jack, though, that made me trust him, least of all the fact that the Amish woman on the bus had spoken highly of him. He had not had time to get hold of her himself—I doubt he had even seen her since she had returned to the family, to her way of life, and yet he had an air of understanding about him. A friend once made was one he would help, even through their friends, if he was able to.

For the next hour, we drank coffee, the taste indescribably bad and yet somehow managing to perk my spirit up. Even if Jack could not help me, even if he walked away from me right then, I had come so far, I knew I could go further.

I found myself asking why I was able to talk to Jack and the woman of the Greyhound bus so freely. The strange young man whose hand I'd held as we travelled from Cleveland to Pittsburgh—I'd given him nothing of myself, just a cover story, an anonymous girl he would forget. Yet others I told as much truth as I dared; to Jack, I told all.

Was it trust? I don't know, but something about those blue eyes and the hidden sorrow that came through each time he smiled or asked a question…I knew that I had belief!

The coffee and the sandwich were finished, so was my interview. We both stood, and I went to shake his hand in a way that said I was OK, I could find a bed for the night around here, even make my way to the airport and hang around the departure lounge. At least I would have the company of strangers to keep me awake and alert until I met up with Catherine.

He shook his head and smiled quizzically. "So, do you want to come back to the bar and talk more? I have a couple of members of staff looking after it for the day." This Englishman was inviting me to stay; I made a promise I would write the Amish woman to express my gratitude.

We walked from the coffee house on 79th Street for a couple of blocks before turning down towards 77th Street. It was there I was introduced to his home, a bar he had worked at since the early eighties when he had left Britain to sink in its own abyss. Now he owned the bar, he lived above it with his on-off girlfriend, never quite making it official, nearly always full of other people who had come seeking light against the shade. I was taken aback by the appearance, of the homeliness of it all, a pool table off to one side, sports pennants and memorabilia lined up behind it, a television tuned to some sort of horse race that was going on somewhere in the world. At the other side of the room was a series of large posters placed in ornately fashioned frames. A couple I recognised: Jon Bon Jovi striking a manly but welcoming pose that would surely have some of the customers dreaming good thoughts after several glasses of wine and beer. Next to it was a picture I didn't quite like at first but which Jack proclaimed his favourite, and then a black-and-white picture which had a topless man with his back turned towards the viewer, the phrase *Broadway Melody of 74* emblazoned above it. Jack told me he had painted that one himself. I had to congratulate him; it was beautiful, alluring, and reminded me of the reason I was heading to Paris.

I asked about the picture I wasn't fond of. Jack said he was a huge fan of the work of a British artist called Mark Wilkinson who had created a series of album covers for a band Jack loved. I felt disturbed by it yet myself drawn to the intricacy of the two figures on display, a soldier and what I took to be Death, although it could have been a shadow of a cardinal, the ambiguity of force and favour being presented, the subtle use of the ace of spades in the left hand, the right hand around the soldier's neck, drawing him into Death's embrace while his dead eyes focused on the offer made.

Whatever image of the passing of time I may have had, this now became a symbol, and in that moment I realised that it was not just French art I liked; it was all art. The depths of a person's soul can be reached if we can place ourselves at the heart of the painting. For too long I had been snobby about art, and I had completely missed the point: art exists everywhere, from the graffiti on a subway wall to the album covers created…even drawn by a strange boy from England whose hand I had held.

Jack and I talked long into the night. For my part, I had questions about his life, how he became a friend to the Amish and why he had come to America. To me, he only asked the simplest of questions, including did I want to see something of New York before I left. I smiled and replied that if I have only one day then I would like to see The Statue of Liberty; it seemed fitting. Jack excused himself and went downstairs; he came back about ten minutes later and clapped his hands as if he'd struck the deal of a lifetime. The two staff members had agreed to work for the next couple of days so he could take me across on the ferry to the island, and the day after to the airport. It was the least he could do for a friend.

The ferry was everything that the subway wasn't. I could almost feel the natural light digging into my bones. The change of pace, the good night's sleep and fresh clothes—I had borrowed some from one of Jack's staff—made a huge difference to my outlook. When the ferry docked, I could not help but walk as close to the base of the giant plinth from which the statue regally gazed across the bay. I turned to take in her view, and what I saw filled me with desire. I saw escape, the start of freedom; I was in control of my destiny, and somewhere across the ocean, my sister was coming for me.

We went back to the mainland and stopped in Battery Park to sit and rest and watch the squirrels shoot up and down the trees. For the first time in my life, I felt completely at ease…until I saw a young man with albinism walking towards me. I had never seen a person with that complexion before, and I am ashamed to say my response was not the best. In fact, it was downright rude.

In childhood, we are taught many things that stick with us, waiting until we can confront those 'truths' with an experience of our own. My father had told he had been cursed by a woman with albinism one night in a bar near our home. That curse, he said, made him hit out in fear at my sister. He swore he didn't know she was pregnant; it was just in response to what the albino had said to him.

Of course, I know now it was bullshit. He was going to lose his best customers if she carried to full term, and he certainly didn't want another child in the house. Still, it made me react badly to this person who only wanted change for the ferry.

Jack didn't have to give me a reproving glance. I felt the shame and embarrassment for us all. I dug deep in my purse and gave the man the change, apologising for my initial half-crazed stare and step back in horror from him. The young man waved it off, smiling, saying it was not the worst he had ever encountered. If anything, that made the experience worse, and after he departed, Jack took my hand without looking at my face, and I felt the agony rip through him. I knew now what had disturbed me about the poster in the bar: it was the bleached-out faces of both Death and the soldier.

That night, Jack took me to a blues bar just down the street. We ate and drank; we listened to music until gone midnight. I could finally laugh about the unfortunate end to our trip to Liberty Island. Such was the scale of the day, I was starting to wonder if my newfound sense of freedom was down to the thought of leaving the country, whether it was because of Jack, or—more likely—because of the city. The subway still made me anxious, but Jack helped me through it, showing me how to be part of the system without giving an inch to those who might make the journey awkward.

A girl can get lost in New York…or she can die there. A part of me understood the words spoken in earnest just a few days ago on the Greyhound bus. The other part didn't care.

In that moment, as I looked up at a sky blistered red by the sinking sun, I knew, despite it all, I'd had the best day of my life.

But days come to an end, and so does life. I am leaving my journal here with Jack. I don't want to take it with me to Paris. It is a memoir of my first years condensed into one short expression of fear and a glimpse of joy. It is not a treasure to keep, rather to share, and I have nothing better to give Jack to say thank you for helping me in these past couple of days than something he can read, to know me as best as he can.

Soon, I shall be in my sister's arms. Jack has asked me to stay, it was all a matter of fact. He said he didn't want me to leave without seeing everything he could show me—so much energy, a pulse of life that goes against all I know. He is insistent, but kind. I sense he is itching to tell me I won't enjoy Paris now that I have tasted New York, that I won't fit in. I am confident he has no romantic designs for me; he likes helping people, perhaps a little too much. Anybody can take in a stray, give it a bed for a night, but you cannot expect it to adhere to your rules straight away. It still feels the feral beat, the urge to piss in a corner of the room rather than go out in the cold, to bite back when the temper turns.

I close the book on this part of my life forever, leave my dad and Cleveland behind me, and I feel good about it.

Chapter Twenty-Two

The Apparent Death of Samantha Ó Foghladh

(Part Two)

HOME SWEET HOME, back on American soil, the land of the brave and the almighty dollar. It is good to be back. Nothing has changed. Everything remains the same—except everything has altered, and nothing is the same as it once was.

I have walked back into a nightmare. I don't know what the future will bring, but right here and now, half strung out with avoiding the attention of a man with clammy, dirty hands and a mouth reeking of two-week-old garbage, I can say with some degree of certainty that America has become the land of the free and easy-going. The handcart to hell is full, so we have borrowed the neighbour's dumpster, put wheels on it and called it a sedan.

I have become the image of my own destruction. If I thought walking away from Montmartre and contemplating suicide at the edge of the Seine was rock bottom, I was sorely mistaken. For here in this crappy room, surrounded by bed bugs, lice and the nightly invasion of cockroaches, not even a bed to my name but a mattress covered in shit and blood—not mine—are my least depressing nightmare. I have reached the seventh circle, and that sedan made out of a dumpster…well, that's going to keep on driving.

I have been locked in this house for a couple of months now, and because I won't sleep with my captor—or *my guardian,* as he would have me call him; once, he even asked me to call him husband—then the penance for the sin of believing I could change my sister's life, as I had changed mine, is firmly in place.

If I want to piss, there is a bucket in the corner; if I want to crap, then hey, the same bucket serves two purposes. My latest rebellion, which saw me serve a week's imprisonment in this attic room, was to spit in his face while a customer was in the kitchen perusing the latest merchandise fresh in from Florida. He ordered me to make him a cup of coffee and to ask nicely if the customer would like one, and I spat right in his face—got him in the left eye. The customer nearly pissed himself laughing, right up until I spat at him too, revelling briefly in watching the slimy, snot-filled glob slither down his open-mouthed face.

I received a black eye for that, and that was from the customer. Men are such cowards, such small-thinking children. As if a black eye was going to get me to cooperate! Not even the threat of pumping me full of drain cleaner would get me to be civil, demure, polite. If I die, I die a free woman. It is the death I deserve after killing my sister.

There is no light up here, save for the sunlight that seldom shines through the narrow cracks in the roof. I have no idea what is going on outside the house, and while I hear the occasional snatch of a voice talking loudly in the kitchen, or the moments of laughter as the drugs take their effect, I hear no phone calls, no messages from Marshall ordering Wells to let me go and put me back on a plane to Paris.

One day, I am going to put a knife through that man's heart.

Being locked in the attic affords me time to think, chained as I am to the wall on the furthest side from the street, the restraint just long enough to get me to the mattress—should I ever sink so low as to sleep on it—and to the bucket. I will say this for Wells: he knows I am still valuable; even as a hostage, he brings me a meal every day and empties the slop bucket each night, always with a look of contempt on his face.

Wells tells me Marshall believes I have been unfaithful, that my demands for help are such that he no longer trusts my loyalty to him. I am putting my own needs above his, above the company he has chosen for me. Wells says that in time Marshall will forgive me, and when the heat has died down and the police stop looking for me—for my sister's murderer—then I can go back to Paris, my sins absolved. Marshall will welcome me back with open arms and I will regain my place at his side. Fuck Marshall. I will return, if only to put a bullet in that smug face of his.

Of all the things to be punished for…

***

I didn't mean to kill my sister. It was the silliest of accidents. If I had meant to kill her, I would have made a far better job of it. I would not have just caught her off-balance and seen her smash her head against the ground.

The flight from Paris had been horrendous. An hour or two earlier and I would have been in the lap of luxury. With a small drink on my table, a good book to read and the thought of seeing my sister again, I would have been in heaven. The initial turbulence should have been an indication of what was to come: by the time we were halfway across the Atlantic, we had been tossed about so badly I thought we might be forced to land in Greenland.

The weather cleared up around fifty miles out of New York, but by then the damage had been done. I don't believe in omens, I don't have faith in God nor conviction that the devil exists, but if that journey was meant to prove anything, it was that somewhere in Paris, Marshall had started to plot against me. I might not believe in the devil, but I do have a strong, unshakable conviction that he is the closest thing to it. I have seen him inject cocaine straight into the tongue of someone who was skimming a percentage off the merchandise. It might not seem a big deal, but when that coke is laced with rat poison and ant powder, well, there are times when I close my eyes and all I can see is that man's pain.

I arrived in America determined to do the right thing. I had gotten Samantha this far; I had a new passport for her in my bag and some ready cash to buy another ticket. After all, the one she had saved from being stolen was worthless without that original passport. I would hold her close, smell her hair, tease her gently about worrying me so, and then we would get her out of America forever.

***

I am back in the attic again, chained up like a rabid dog, only this time I cannot reach the bucket to relieve myself. Foaming at the mouth through lack of water, I am feeling the depths of exhaustion, and sharing a bloodstained mattress occupied by lice is tempting, but I resolve not to let this bastard break me. I just have to wait, bide my time. At least now I know where he keeps the machine for making false passports.

I keep seeing her head hit the ground. I replay it over and over again in my mind, and I hear the man she was with yelling at me, *"What have you done? What have you done?"* What have I done?

I saw her sitting at that table, a glass of water in front of her. She looked tired and pale, a sliver of concern etched on the face of the man sitting next to her. I didn't know who he was, but I felt a chill run down my spine. Something was wrong. Was she pregnant? I could not take her to Paris if she was. She was meant to become educated—how could she do that with a baby to provide for?

I approached the table, a big smile on my face, the false premise of the meeting had begun. The closer I got, the more I realised that my original suspicion was off the mark. She wasn't pregnant; something else troubling her. Perhaps she'd had second thoughts. Perhaps this man had convinced her to stay. Maybe he had threatened her; she was not as strong as me. I considered her still a child, mentally. Physically, she was every bit the gawky teenager—awkward, uncomfortable in her body, tongue-tied and ill at ease with confrontation.

I took the initiative and started the dance between us by asking the man, whoever he was, if he wouldn't mind giving us privacy, assuredly pointing out that his job was done, thank you very much, but we didn't need him anymore.

Samantha held his hand tight, looked at me with as much defiance as she could muster, and told him to stay. She forcibly told me that he was the reason she was there; she had only gotten this far thanks to this man, who I learned was called Jack, and his friends. Then her face took on a pained expression, and she doubled over. Stomach cramps, she said.

I attempted to drag her away, only succeeding in ripping her purse out of her sweaty hands. I heard Jack's voice, muffled but full of riotous anger, a sense of protection welling up from deep inside. She went to stand, her beautiful eyes swam away with her mind, and her legs gave way, her body following the same path. And as she went down, her head hit the side of the table then the ground, and her eyes closed.

***

I have played at being good, or is it that I have become compliant, willing to see the world from Wells' position? I have not been locked away for a month now, and yesterday I went out into the yard. At least, I think I did. It might have been the day before, when I was introduced to a new lover, someone who made the clouds roll away and left me seeing new colours in the dullness. My thoughts echo; the sound of chatter and confusion is a constant aural blur. Occasionally, I can pick out a voice, sirens, hyperventilating, keep calm, she fell, but you were there, sirens, no, Officer, not seen that woman around here, I am here in the attic, chains, a prisoner, I am out here, melting into the ground, there is fire, my veins they are boiling, a man in a uniform stops me, are you all right, Miss? I run past him,

keep my head low, lower, must find a phone booth, must contact…
must contact…him.

***

I was out of it for two weeks. The withdrawal was agony;
the pain was like nothing I had ever felt before. Being punched in
the stomach when I was pregnant—I thought at the time I could
not feel anything as horrific as that, but this was misery with
a soul, the torment of a thousand demons ripping open my gut
and Wells looking for all the world as if he was going to puke and
shit himself with fear.

I am back in the attic again, but this time I have not been
chained up. The old mattress was taken away one afternoon and
a new one replaced it, clean sheets brought in. I was dressed in a
tasteless yellow nightgown—I guessed the clothes I had been in
for a while had been taken to the same place as the lice-infested
mattress—and while I could not speak to her, I noticed an old
woman cleaning around me, laying down traps. Wells stood
on the other side of the room, his demeanour changed, almost
repentant. The woman kept raising her voice at him, ordering
him to fetch things, to make soup. I didn't understand a word
being said, but the actions spoke volumes.

I still couldn't escape, but I had company while I withdrew
from whatever Wells had put inside me. She sat with me.
She cleaned my sick bucket. She helped me with the cramps, the
fever, and to go to the toilet downstairs, then helped me back
into bed again. She fed me, mothered me, cared for me in a
way I had never been cared for. Then one day, she disappeared,
and I had Wells for company. I had no strength in my body to
take him on.

Two days later, the old lady returned. It made me smile when
she berated him, slapping him around the head. I asked how long
I had been in the building. The old lady looked at Wells with some
distress, and he hung his head in shame. Almost seven months,
he admitted.

Most women would have exploded with rage, and rightly so. They would have gone in and buried their nails deep into the flesh of their captor, shredding the face of the one who had kept them away from the world until they looked as if they had been attacked by a mountain lion, the scars that never truly heal, deep and penetrating. I just sat there numb, confused. In all that time, nobody had missed me. What had Marshall told people? How had he explained my disappearance?

The old lady smiled and held up a bag, urging me to look inside. New clothes: a couple of decent-looking skirts, bit young for me but they would fit; new underwear; a couple of tops. There was also a pair of scuffed-up sneakers. The woman said something I didn't understand, and as Wells interpreted, I realised it was the first proper and kind sentence he had said to me since the day he had opened the door and told me Marshall would call me by the end of the night. "She is sorry. She didn't know if you were a hose or stockings woman. She hopes socks will do."

I wanted to cry. How pathetic—to feel gratitude towards someone who has treated you so badly, who has forced you into chains, given you drugs against your will and neglected you. But this was how my life started out under my father's roof. I had tried so hard to gain his affections, and he found ways to abuse me, turned me into his joke, the butt to be passed around, like a blunt at a freshman's party, each one shooting their load on me.

***

I fled the departure lounge, I remember now. There were no shouts of 'stop' from Jack, perhaps too stunned to do anything but see to Samantha as she lay dying. I stopped and collected my thoughts: *call Marshall, tell him everything.*

He sounded busy, preoccupied. I asked him where he was, and he joked with me that he was at JFK, taking in the scenery. I hated him for that. He knew I was freaking out, and he compounded it by making stupid jokes. Inside my sister's purse, there was money, a small amount of make-up, a small notebook in which she had scribbled down a few sentences, including an address of someone called Ash in England, and a tape, not even an official album, some kind of knock-off homemade piece of shit. I was about to throw it in the trash but thought better of it.

I could still hear Marshall talking and an announcement going on in the background which muffled most of what he said to me. I listened again and took another look inside the tape's casing—not a bad drawing, on reflection. There was a small note: *Don't forget to let me know that you have made it to Paris, Ash.*

I stared at it, no idea what to do, but Marshall was ending the call, so I acted without thought, said, "You need to send a letter to a man named Ash in England, here is the address. Make it realistic and nice—just say she has arrived in Paris but that she doesn't want to see him again."

As Wells and I headed out of the city, my first steps I had taken out of the house for eight months, I thought deeply about that moment. I found myself understanding why Marshall had punished me. It wasn't because of the money or the tickets; he knew I would have paid him back within a week. It was because I was the fly in his soup that he couldn't digest, so he found someone else to eat me instead. He had passed me over.

If I hadn't told him about the letter, all would have been well.

Wells swore. Damn radio, nothing but static. I looked in my bag, not that I had much in there. He still wouldn't trust me with any cash. I pulled out the tape I had taken from my sister and told him to put it on, I could do with a memory. It made the journey to New Jersey more bearable, and for the first time, I felt Wells relax. *Come as you are...as you want me to be...*

Chapter Twenty-Three

Secrets, Lies and Audiotape

The Captain Finishes the Job

B Y DISCHARGING MYSELF from the hospital, I knew I had waived any rights I may have had under my insurance policy to receive treatment, but some things are bigger than life. That was the way I saw it, as I lay there with tubes poking out of me, my wife staring at me in accusation—*how dare you survive!*—caught between wanting me to recover and switching off the machines that may or may not have been keeping me alive. I wish I could have told her it was all right, I deserved such apathy, such disdain, but instead, I took it as a cue to fight one last time.

I am not sure if it was a sense of glee or admiration for perseverance which I saw reflected in her eyes. I wouldn't be surprised if it was just the glint of my phone screen flashing away with the series of calls and text messages that still demanded my attention. I could have walked away from the police at that moment, begged forgiveness from my long-suffering wife and found a way to repair the damage wrought over the last thirty years, but to hell with her. When it came down to it, I had to maintain the law, even at my own expense.

I got off the bed, even that was painful, but it felt good to be in command of my own life again. The look of disdain on my wife's face said it all, but she reiterated anyway: "Leave now and it is over between us. I shall not come back for you again."

I took her hand, perhaps for the first time in a decade, and looked deep into her eyes. I studied those years in the accumulation of lines, in the acid tongue behind teeth clamped in harboured resentment, and I realised I didn't care. Not for her; not for my position; not for my life.

It was with some satisfaction that, as I let go of her hands, I didn't tell her to go fuck herself. I just smiled and told her she will be happy again one day.

Unsure of what had just happened, she just stood there, open goldfish mouth and narrow snake eyes. I located my uniform, took off my gown and allowed the full spectacle of too many years behind a desk to be hammered home in a vision that my wife would not see again. "The least you can do as a final goodbye is allow me to dress in peace and not as if I'm auditioning for a peep show." I enjoyed that. It had gotten her to close her mouth anyway.

But rather than the words hitting her in the way I had intended, the hope that I might see her walk out of my life instead of me walking out of hers, she insisted on helping me with my shirt, made sure my tie was tidy and that I hadn't forgotten my suspenders. She tsked at the lack of polish on my shoes, and I smiled, said, "I don't think it matters anymore."

Picking up my phone, I noted the missed calls from Catherine and my colleague in the Maltese police. I put it in my pocket and held out my hand to my wife. She took it. It was a moment of odd serenity that we hadn't experienced for most of our marriage, but then one expects peace when the war is over. I said goodbye and thank you. I meant it. In return, she smiled, and replied, "Thank you for the house. It will raise funds for the church." Damn woman, always with the last kick to the balls.

A couple of doctors tried to stop me from walking out of the hospital—I had just had a cardiac arrest, I needed to stay. Their concern was touching, but so was the help into the squad car by two young officers who had just dropped off a drunk driver who had crashed his car into a ditch. Typical, really. It is a crime I truly cannot stand, and on any other night, I would have delighted in hearing them read him his rights. Instead, I told them to call another unit to take care of it. Nobody would know tonight, there were bigger fish to fry. I gave them the address where we would find Catherine Ó Foghladh, and I settled into the back seat and waited for the inevitable question on my health.

I told them that sometimes police gossip harder than the fishwives of old, that it was a wonder I wasn't dead and buried and my funeral had already taken place. "Nothing to it, boys, a spot of indigestion—you'll have to stop feeding me doughnuts, or better still, get the arrest figures up."

I knew they were not convinced, and in a way I was grateful. I hoped I had fostered a different generation of police officers in Cleveland, ones not corrupted by the old ways, of envelopes and looking the other way when the time calls. At least this showed I had their sympathy, which might come in handy later when the job was done and my own justice was served.

The office Catherine worked out of was the only one aside from the lobby where there were lights blazing. We gained entry to the building with ease: it turned out that Catherine was as good as her word. Her message to me was sharp, formal and reeked of fury and provocation.

As the two officers and I stepped onto the elevator, I took a moment to listen to the calls I had missed from the detective in Malta. It seemed an odd request, but in the short time I had come to know him, I found I trusted him more than most, and that included Catherine, to whom my eyes had been opened, the scales not just falling away but replaced with suspicion, uncertainty and misgivings.

I put my phone away and felt a twinge of pain. I reached into my pocket and took out the pills I had been given, swallowing them dry, the aftertaste bitter, the reaction in my stomach unpleasant, but the sweetness of the brief relief gave me hope that

I might see this through. I instructed the men by my side to take note of everything, no matter how uncomfortable it became, no matter what was said about me, to use it all in evidence.

The elevator stopped smoothly. I wasn't keen on modern elevators, all closed in and restrictive. I grew up in an era when it was fashionable to see the metal casing around you, the ornate skeleton giving you a view of what was to come, no sudden surprises.

The door opened efficiently and with no regard for fuss. The open-plan office presented itself, clean, ordered, no sign of a tornado having yet touched down on Catherine Ó Foghladh's life, no chaos of emotions scattered in its wake. Instead, there was soft jazz playing in the background, wordless, an arrangement that left pinpricks in your heart. 'Nuclear Waltz', I think it was called. A 1970s piece. Eyes opened, a stirring memory, I could not place it, but it wasn't the first time I had heard this particular piece of music. It made no difference; there was a job to do.

The chair behind the oak desk turned, and Catherine made her entrance, embodying the evil men who sought to fashion the world in their own image across scores of films. They all had this trait, the person who had concocted the elaborate plan slowly revealing their true nature to the audience. What made this more disturbing, more stomach-churning, was that Catherine was dressed as a younger woman. She had on a red wig, and when she stood, the short skirt rose just that little higher. Her make-up was that of under-confidence embellished—this was not the appearance of a woman on the shoulders of turning fifty; this was a haunting from the past. I swallowed hard and understood; the game had been playing out far longer than I had realised.

Noticing she had my full attention, she simply smiled and held up a jacket for the officers to see. It was the jacket of the young woman I had not arrested all those years ago, young on the beat, full of optimism and good nature.

My mouth became dry as I struggled to form a sentence, the pain in my chest reminding me of all I was about to lose—

a far greater realisation than that of thirty minutes before, when I had told my wife goodbye. I managed to say, "You told me you were eighteen. You said your name was Lorraine. I even met your roommate."

Her laughter was cruel, deserved. I thought back to the time when she had shown her gratitude against my better concerns, and I felt sick. She put the jacket on the chair and walked around the desk, one finger placed in mock seduction on her bottom lip.

"Did you hear that, Officers? He thought I was eighteen. Anything else that gets said tonight, I want you to remember this with greater clarity. I was *fifteen*. I was pregnant with your child, and that woman who was my roommate? She was a prostitute I knew because of my father, the man whose death you never really investigated until now."

I had never felt shame like this before. I had screwed up, but I had to keep my emotions in check. There was still time to put it right.

I watched her remove the wig, her natural colour shining through. She tore off her short skirt, and one of the officers turned away. This was a turn-on for her. The prim and proper saviour of the city had been reduced to her true nature, a feral wildcat protecting her territory. She walked over to the coat rack and removed from one of the hooks a long, black skirt and proceeded to put it on, making sure the two of us watching her every move were given free rein of our imaginations.

As she fastened the zipper, slowly pulling it, both hands behind her back as if she were handcuffed to the clothing, I walked over to her desk and turned my back on her. I started searching the area the Maltese detective had told me to look and found it almost immediately: a tape, homemade.

"I like a bit of Nirvana myself," I lied. I turned back to face Catherine, who had now removed the school-like blouse and was putting on a black, silky high-end shirt, each button elegantly pressed through its hole. She had no idea what I was talking about, hadn't realised that in my hand was the one piece of evidence tying her to her sister. She continued to dress, a long black coat wrapping her against the cold to come.

I said, "Tell me about Baldomero Wells."

She stopped, arms half in the coat. I had taken her by surprise; her grin faded.

"Tell me about your sister—the one I have been searching for all this time."

She started to protest, not about the man in New York, but about her sister. I showed her the tape. She had obviously kept it with her as a reminder, a memento...a trophy. I signalled to the officer closest to the stereo to pull the plug on the music. It was a distraction, and I wanted her to focus completely on me, on the accusations.

There was anger in my voice when I asked her again about her sister. I'd had enough of the absurd game of chess playing out in this office. She stared at me with pure hatred and tried to turn the conversation back to me, stammering that she had lost the baby when her father had hit her in the stomach, that she regretted the last few years of working with me, albeit that it amused her to think one of Cleveland's top policeman had been with her every day and not realised she was the one he'd had underage sex with—"They have words for that. You're going to jail, Captain Holt."

She urged the other two officers to arrest me, but they stood firm, good men, allowing this charade to play out. I knew I would avoid jail; the pain in my chest would deliver me straight to hell.

"Tell me about Baldomero Wells," I asked once more. "Tell me about Abigael Wells."

She picked up a hat, the kind that could have adorned the head of a movie star, a black trilby with a red feather in it. Putting it on, she turned slightly to look at her reflection in the long, wooden-framed mirror and adjusted the hat to a rakish angle, her hair flowing down the back of the coat. I mused aloud that she should have kept the wig on. It would have given her the look she was so desperate to achieve. Finally, she placed a pin through the hat to keep it in place. She was ready for her audition.

Hands in her pockets, she shrugged in that time-honoured gesture: *There is nothing to tell, I don't know who you mean.*

I took a step towards her, held aloft the tape. She made a grab for it. We both knew I had her on this alone, but then she also had me, the vice-like grip of our hands a testament to the sheer lengths to which we were both prepared to go.

"I think this would be better off at the station." I motioned to one of the officers to read her her rights and instructed the other to read me mine. There was sorrow in his eyes as he did so. There are lots of bad men out there who prey on such girls— evil, disgusting men—and he could see by her alluding to having lied to me about her age that I was only guilty of naivety. But what does that matter? I was guilty. Some will argue I had abused my position, and they are probably right, although I wouldn't let Catherine see it. I knew the police force would be shaken by this.

Slowly, she withdrew her left hand from her pocket and raised it towards me, a small gun glinting in the light of the room. She smiled at me with a mixture of triumph and dashing, and for a brief, tangible moment, I saw the young woman caught in the office of the games arcade, the illusion she chose to create. If I was evil for my crime, then what did that make her? I had no words. I had placed my trust in this woman. I had allowed myself to believe that the future of the city was safe with her, but she had turned out exactly like her old man. There was blood on her hands, and she was willing to spill more. A smile from a serpent is still a smile.

She turned the gun away from me and pointed it at her temple. I heard the two officers tell her to put it down.

I had never known Catherine to carry a gun, and I believe she would have carried it through, killed herself rather than admitting her guilt. I took a calculated risk: I walked towards her, much to the dismay of the two young officers, and put the tape in my pocket. I tried to convey to her that we both were in trouble but this was not the way to deal with it, it wouldn't bring her sister back. I accepted I was going to end the night either as a stiff on a mortician's table or in jail, hopefully the latter. Shouldn't she accept the same? That if she killed herself to avoid jail, it would send out the wrong signal and undo all the good she had done?

I don't know if my words meant anything at all, but she lowered the gun and let it drop to the floor, this broken woman who had fought back as hard as she could, resigned to the understanding that in the end, fate knows how to play chess better than any of us.

Chapter Twenty-Four

How Catherine Ó Foghladh Killed Her Captor

A Statement

BALDOMERO WELLS HAD everything coming to him, so when he finally got word from Marshall that I was to return to Paris, that Wells was to create a new passport and identity for me, I spent my time being the best captive I could be. I became, for a short but invaluable time, the best friend he'd ever had.

I had already wormed my way into his mind, allowed him to think he was in control of me. Now all I needed to do was find the money I knew he had stashed in the house. In his kitchen, the meeting room for all his deals, two guns were hidden. The shipment of coke came in once a week, at nine in the morning, wrapped in the stuffing of small teddy bears—I had seen the old woman parcelling it up, tying dainty red bows around their necks, a smile of satisfaction on her face. I don't think she knew what the teddy bears contained. I think she just liked helping Wells, like some sort of mother figure—why else would she have helped him to clean me up and insisted that he take me to New Jersey?

That evening on the beach was the most unrestricted I had been for some time. Even though it didn't last, it was a sign that my mind was still working. We had driven for around ninety minutes, getting out of New York quite quickly and heading down into New Jersey. There were boxes in the back of the car—uppers, downers, heroin, coke—did it matter when there was a huge party going on and money to be made from students having their final blowout of the season?

I had started to feign interest in the business, or maybe it wasn't a mask. Maybe I smelled opportunity and didn't know it at that precise moment. Whatever, it's not important. What concerns you is how I killed Wells.

The catalyst was that party. I saw someone on the other side of the fire who stared at me continuously for half an hour. I thought at first it was someone who recognised me from Cleveland—perhaps I was still being hunted in connection with my sister's death—and instantly I felt hemmed in again, trapped. The innocent persona I had affected for the evening's work took hold of me, made me fearful of the flickers of the bonfire's flame, the shadows dancing menacingly, and I started to panic.

All the while Wells was ingratiating himself to the crowd, I was trying to avoid the eyes of the stranger on the other side of that fire. When he became distracted by the person next to him, I took my chance to slip into the darkness. I stumbled across the New Jersey sand and pebbles towards the water, feeling the heat of the flames ebb away from me, the sense of wretchedness flow over me. I could have walked out into the ocean, taken one last breath and let myself go, but as you have already gathered, I may threaten suicide, but I am not that brave. Nobody takes my life, not even me.

From behind me, I heard footsteps, and then someone grabbed my shoulder. They were shouting my sister's name, insisting that I was her. Wells came into view and started swinging out at the figure, telling my assailant to keep their hands of his wife. I was still too far gone to argue that I belonged to no one. I never have, not even your dear captain. Not even Marshall. But it seemed to do the trick. The unknown person came to a standstill and then lunged for Wells' shirt pocket. He pulled out the tape I had given

Wells to play in the car and then started raving again like a mad man. He was relentless and kept saying, "Samantha, Samantha, it's me!"

Wells snatched back the tape just as some of the other partygoers came rushing over. Whoever this man was, he was fairly popular with them, and they rounded on Wells, started shoving him, telling him to go home, that we were not wanted there—"Who invited you anyway?" "It's the guy selling the pills, man."

All the time this was going on, I watched the mystery figure carefully. He had more guts than I did—he started to walk into the cold ocean, the last rays of the sun reflecting his pain, enhanced by the lights of the police boat in the distance.

Wells and I were manhandled away from the scene, sworn at, told to get lost. I remember Wells taking a swing at one of the young partygoers but missing completely. Back at the car, Wells lashed out, thundering and cursing in his native tongue. We drove around the block a couple of times, him all the while thumping the steering wheel. It was a couple of hours later before he calmed down enough to tell me that the evening had been a total waste of time. He'd hoped to make nearly a hundred thousand dollars that night, but after paying for the shipment and the middle man, he'd be left with barely enough to cover the effort of going.

I stayed silent, nodding in the right places. I was thinking. When he stopped ranting, I pointed out that this wasn't going to be the only party on a beach tonight and suggested we move further along the coast, head down into Wildwood. He wouldn't make the money he wanted to, but with my expertise at business gained at Marshall's side, he would still make a profit. I would help him sell, I could be persuasive, and I said, hoping he would take it as a joke, "You look like a drug dealer. I, on the other hand, look good enough to have sex with. Sometimes you have to sell yourself to make money."

I could almost see the cogs whirring, the steam coming out of his ears as he ran the idea through his mind. It's funny how you men think with that tiny muscle, but it didn't take long for Wells to understand how good my idea was. That night, we made a killing. Not only did we come close to making the money he wanted, but we sold out of everything that was in the trunk of the car. It was clean. We were just Mr. and Mrs. Wells out for a drive, enjoying the last of our vacation time, honeymooners if anyone asked.

My idea worked so well that he began to trust me more. I even left the house unattended a couple of times. I didn't go far; I just wanted to find my way to the closest subway station; my plan was forming.

I worked for my freedom. I blew Baldomero every chance I got. I took advantage of the concern he showed to the old woman, and one day when she was sick, I wrapped up the boxes, even making sure the delicate bow signature she placed on each one was visible and tied in the way I had seen her do it a hundred times. I am a quick learner, especially when I know I can turn it to my advantage.

The time for me to leave presented itself when Wells received the call from Marshall. I was to return to Paris—had I learned my lesson? Most certainly. I knew where Wells kept the money he'd collected over the previous week. I had rarely been seen, so few people had taken notice of me, especially when Wells was ready to slap them away. I had already gotten my sister's tape back; I just needed the cash and the means of escape.

There are those who plan meticulously, who see the world as a series of hurdles not to be jumped but to be examined in minute detail. But sometimes you just need a moment to swing your way and the future can be yours.

I persuaded the old woman to take a personal day, to go and get me some more clothes from downtown. Wells was more than happy with the arrangement. What man can resist the temptation of beer, dope and red-hot sex? For that was what I offered brazenly. It was the last thing he accepted with a grin.

This was not an alleyway trap. I wasn't the young woman I had been. I still retained my beauty and charm, despite Wells' best efforts to destroy them both when I had initially come to the house in search of sanctuary. I believed I had a couple of hours in which to settle the score, to get the money together, to take the passport Wells had created that morning and to get as far away as possible.

JFK would have been a stupid move, so would Newark. I would have to travel to Washington D.C.—it would be the best option. Time was of the essence. I kissed Wells with what he thought was passion—your captain will understand that. It doesn't take a lot to convince a man that you love them. I took Wells right there in the kitchen. I made sure he was completely sated, and then, using a knife I had stowed in the belt loops of my skirt, I tore through his neck swiftly and without missing a beat of my heart.

Revenge is always best when you have been eagerly awaiting the thrill. I moved away from his slow-twitching body, and for a minute I watched him struggle to breathe, to stay alive. As he placed his hands over his neck, I kicked over the chair he was sitting on and upended the table. I took another chair and smashed it against the floor. All the while, I watched his face, contorting, twisting in pain in the final seconds of his life. Finally, I picked up the remaining chair, and with no remorse or sound from my lips, I smashed it over his dead body, splinters of wood embedding themselves in his face.

I retrieved the knife and washed it thoroughly, scrubbing my hands and then the sink. Wells had become careless around me. I didn't need much encouragement to spy, to keep my mouth shut, or open when the need arose. I walked with purpose to where I had seen him put the money, gathered up the passport and the recently washed knife, then, just for kicks, I went back to the prone body of Baldomero Wells and looked down into his blank, expressionless eyes. I smiled. It was great to be alive. For good measure, I took one of the guns from their respective hideaways and positioned it in his hand. I made it look like a struggle, a deal gone wrong.

If I had been stopped, I would have just said I was a prostitute. "The knife? Well, a girl's got to have protection, Officer!" It would have meant jail, but at least there I would not have been forced to blow a man for my freedom. I was worrying over nothing; no one saw me leave the house—nobody had really known I was there except for the old woman, and I doubt she would have said anything. She might even have stayed away from the house once she realised it had been turned over by someone else, and assumed that in the madness, I had escaped. The poor girl she had cared for, treated as one of her own, had managed to flee and would now be hiding somewhere. Women like her know when to call it a day.

I bought some clothes in various shops along the way, using a restroom to change, disposing of the knife in the Harlem River from the top of the Henry Hudson Bridge. Then I casually walked on, boarded a train and made my way to Washington D.C.

The last time I had been in an airport I had panicked. This time, I showed the world just how calm I could be, not even batting an eyelash when asked for my passport as I handed over the cash for a ticket to Paris.

When I reached Charles de Gaulle, I called Marshall. He was in a good mood: "I believe a mutual friend of ours has been found dead, his throat slit, caught unawares by the hooker he had been… entertaining. His house is ransacked, local police are looking for a rival gang. I do hope you bought me all the money you found in the house, less your cut, of course. I must congratulate you, Catherine. It seems you have learned your lesson after all."

It is important for a woman to survive all that the world can throw at her, to be superior to the effects and ripples of others' stunted minds. After the events of September 11th, I told Marshall

I was leaving for good; I was going back to Cleveland. I had been loyal to his cause, and I remained so. I think he appreciated me not putting a bullet in his head at the first opportunity. I forgave him for his actions that had seen me trapped in New York, but the funny thing is, I have never been able to forgive myself for running out on my sister as she lay dying. The fear of that moment has driven me on.

Yes, I am guilty of murdering Baldomero Wells, but I did not kill my sister—not in the way you mean—and there is still no body. Marshall…I am glad he is dead, but I do miss him. I wish he had gotten to take down that policeman in Malta, though perhaps I should just be satisfied he found the boy who created such a mess for him. He is dead now, what does that even matter?

Am I going to go to court before or after Holt has had his day in the dock? I would so love to hear how many years he receives for statutory rape. I know I told him I was old enough, but he was in a position not only of trust, but one that would have allowed him to check who I was. It's not my fault he believed the lie. If anything good has come out of this, it is the knowledge that he has lost everything. He should have arrested me when he found me in that arcade office. I'm sure my father would have looked kindly on that and put a contract on his head. Nobody screws with the Ó Foghladhs. I hope that Holt remembers that for as long as he lives.

Then again, I'd expected him to remember me before tonight—it says a lot about how his mind works, his perversions only permitting him to recognise me when I dressed up in the guise of someone from his past. Men—you are all the same. You take what must not be taken, you think the world belongs to you, but in the end, women will make you suffer. It's quite fitting that Holt's wife is giving all the money from the house to the church. She deserves a better life than the one he gave her.

They tell me you know who killed my father. I'm just glad it wasn't my sister. I had always suspected it could have been her, pushed too far, threatened with who knows what—knowing my father, I dread to think. He was capable of almost anything.

Will you do me a favour and get a message to Ash Corrish for me? Can you send him back his tape—the one Holt had in his pocket? Let him know it was nothing personal, he was just the best man to take the fall. And tell him he must have been special for my sister to pick him as a shield when she left Cleveland. Tell him…I hope we never meet again.

Epilogue

A Telephone Call

I F ONLY SHE and Captain Holt had ignored the letter to the local newspaper…if Ash Corrish had not felt the need to reconnect with his past, all of this could have been avoided, but they say everything happens for a reason. All I can say is the view from my island doesn't look half bad when I compare it to the storms elsewhere.

The music plays on. Isn't that what always happens at the end of such a story? The sad refrain of a violin sums up the situation, encapsulating the despair and the loss before concluding as a drifting lullaby that confirms what you have seen is just that: a story; another anecdote for the regulars at the bar, gossiping over glasses of cheap bourbon as the sun goes down.

My father used to say that when the sun rises over that hill, you have a chance to live your day anew. I prefer to think of it as when the sun goes down over the sea, you have a chance to forget you ever lived.

I didn't know how to respond when I heard Holt had been charged with corrupting a minor. I read the evidence, and whilst the crime was abhorrent, he truly didn't know she was underage. Such margins wouldn't help him if he went to prison, of course. Given his state of health, I suspected he would be packed off somewhere, but he would always be looking over his shoulder, worrying who was out there, in the dark.

I should not have felt the pangs of melancholia, but it was better than thinking about the problems of the previous two weeks. Ash Corrish had gone back to England. He had to sail to Sicily and then onto Italy, where he would catch a train across the continent before sailing back across the English Channel. The doctors at the hospital would not let him fly, but I believed Rose's wife was joining them in Paris. I wondered if Ash would make a small diversion and place some flowers somewhere nice, somewhere there would always be a memory for him.

He seemed coy about the future. Rose told me he'd received a phone call the night before they sailed but wouldn't tell me who the phone call was from. She just smiled with charm and an enigmatic glow to her face. I hoped he found happiness, although it would be hard, especially as he had to deal with his sister.

I waved them off, my last official duty in this strange case that wasn't really mine until Corrish was beaten up in my police station. The connections we have are greater than we realise: one misplaced word and a whole system can topple. We should be more careful about the reconnections we seek; there is a reason why someone leaves our story.

At least I had found what I hoped was the last bad apple in my own backyard. The constable who let Capone into the building was facing charges, and Capone—well, he wouldn't be seeing daylight for quite some time.

As for Catherine Ó Foghladh and her sister's murder—they could not make the charge stick, but I didn't think she'd killed her. There was only one report of an ambulance turning up at the airport on the day Catherine was there. A young woman was taken to the hospital and found to be suffering from botulism of all things. It was touch and go, but they managed to save her. However, the girl was a Jane Doe and disappeared before an investigation could be started.

I don't believe Samantha is dead, I think she is out there, somewhere.

The Pub seemed more crowded than I remembered, perhaps because I hadn't been there for quite some time. Of course, there was a poetry meeting tonight, and the owner always made them feel welcome. I sat with a beer and a Scotch chaser, next to the empty chair always reserved for Oliver Reed. I smiled at the crowd jostling for space, the cheer of the evening enhanced by the eagerly awaited appearance of the Maltese Songbird, a woman who had gained the reputation she deserved. I had missed this type of company.

As the crowd were about to go upstairs and start their meeting, my phone vibrated: the chief. I gave a watery smile of apology to my host and walked outside into the shade of the street, the jubilation of the evening causing me to move further away from The Pub than I would have liked.

Such phone calls are always a double-edged sword. There is the 'congratulations for a job well done' which inflates your ego, makes you proud of your work, then the prick of the balloon which deflates, collapsing the moment of elation as you realise that the job is never done. Crime, especially murder, never knows when to stop.

Will I take over the investigation of the murdered actress? Not a request; an order from higher up the food chain. Her stage name was Estelle de Gracey, but her true name was Stella Grace Benn, and she was once a student at the University of Liverpool, where one of her guest lecturers had been my old friend.

I lowered my head in the time-honoured salute of the weary and the put-upon, but agreed. I would meet him in the office in the morning. I shifted on my feet, moving smartly out the way of two middle-aged holidaymakers arguing about the best way to get down to the ferry to take them back to Sliema. I almost reached The Pub when my phone went again: an unknown number. There was a time when I would have dismissed such calls, as I had almost done with Holt, but of late I had accepted there were people out there who needed to talk to me but whose numbers I did not know—my son being the main one, but there were others.

I answered the phone. I could hear breathing, steady but shallow, almost upset.

"Hello, Sir. I just want to tell you that I am all right, I am home, and I am with my mother. I can't talk about where I have been yet. I need to rest—may I call you in a couple of days, when I have written up my report?"

My Magpie. She is safe. That was one concern I could put aside for now, although my brain wanted to know where exactly she had been. I didn't ask. I put my phone away and walked back into The Pub, picked up my two drinks, which surprisingly nobody had seen fit to polish off, and took the stairs up to the poetry meeting. I needed a distraction.

Acknowledgements

It felt like a one-off. I had written my detective novel for my father, and whether it was enjoyed or not I leave up to you. For my part, I took the life of the detective with no name seriously. It was the culmination of one of my dreams to see something I had created stand up to people's expectations. I made the conscious decision in January 2019 to scale back on all the reviewing I've had the honour of doing since 2004, my body no longer able to take the pressure of the six-night week of constantly going out. Instead, I made plans for the summer of that year to be one of writing; anything else I had in the bag would be erased.

Dark Chrysalis came out of nowhere. I had considered a return to the Maltese detective, but I couldn't find a way to make him or the story work. Then, one night in May 2019, I re-read a poem I had written to someone I met on a Greyhound bus whilst I travelled around America and Canada as a much younger man. I got to thinking about what may have happened to her after I left the bus in Pittsburgh and she carried onwards to live her own ambitions. Where do people go when you leave their story?

In the modern age, we are able to look up old friends and reconnect, but there are some drawers you don't reopen. You let them remain closed. But what if…what if you were to take a peek, to see the dust that has collected on the drawers of your past and brush them off, clean them down. I found my story, and whilst it remains in the hands of the detective, the jigsaw is not really about him. It is about those connections we make, those that last, those that wither and die, the mistakes we make and the handshakes of insincerity we receive from those who never truly were our friends.

So, old friend, a return in a way to Malta, an island I have come to love but also to other places which have become part of my story. I want to say a huge thank you to the superb Felicity Pryke, Richard and Tracey Waters, my old school friend Justin Brown, my dear adopted sister Paula Turner, Tony Higginson, Bob Stone, Helen Duke, Mark Luker, John Chatterton, Gemma Bodinetz, Carole Labrum, Dennis Riley, the Maltese Songbird Miriam Calleja Shaw, artist extraordinaire Cyrano Denn and Elke Maasbommel for their invaluable support in my writing. Most of all, I would like to thank my ever-encouraging wife Judith and my parents David and Julie Hall. Without these people, as well as others, I would not be here writing to you now.

I would also like to say a huge thank you to the good people at Beaten Track Publishing, especially Debbie McGowan. The world of publishing has become a minefield; it takes someone very special to lead you to safety and give you the space and time to develop. Thank you.

To you, my old friend, wherever you are now, I do hope you got to paint by the Seine.

Ian D. Hall
July 2019

About the Author

Having been found on a 'Co-op' shelf in Stirchley, Birmingham by a Cornish woman and a man of dubious footballing taste, Ian grew up in neighbouring Selly Park and Bicester in Oxfordshire. After travelling far and wide, he now considers Liverpool to be his home.

Ian was educated at Moor Green School, Bicester Senior School, and the University of Liverpool, where he gained a 2:1 (BA Hons) in English Literature.

He now reviews and publishes daily on the music, theatre and culture within Merseyside.

Please visit www.liverpoolsoundandvision.co.uk

By the Author

Tales from the Adanac House
Black Book
The Death of Poetry
Four in the Morning, Pavement Blues
Dark Chrysalis

Beaten Track Publishing

For more titles from Beaten Track Publishing,
please visit our website:

https://www.beatentrackpublishing.com

Thanks for reading!

Printed in Great Britain
by Amazon